CHANNA WICKREMESEKERA

ASYLUM

This is a work of fiction. Names, characters, places, and incidents either are the product of the author's imagination or are used fictitiously. Any resemblance to actual persons, living or dead, events, or locales is entirely coincidental.

ASYLUM
A Palaver Book

For additional information, bulk or educational purchases, and other resources, please contact Ethica Projects, Pty Ltd.

First Palaver edition published September 2015.

Cover illustration and design by Jacob Benjamin.

Publisher's Cataloguing-In-Publication Data:
Wickremesekera, Channa, 1967– author
Asylum / Channa Wickremesekera
ISBN: 978-0-9943431-0-9 (paperback)
ISBN: 978-0-9943431-1-6 (eBook)
1. Interpersonal relations—Fiction. 2. Cultural pluralism—Religious aspects—Islam—Fiction.
3. Religious ethics—Fiction. 4. Teenage boys—Fiction.
5. Family problems—Fiction. 6. Australia—Fiction. I. Title
DDC: A823.4 '223

PALAVER | www.palaver.com
Palaver is an imprint of Ethica Projects, Pty Ltd
10 Barnato Grove, Armadale, Victoria 3143, Australia

To all the people who were good
to me when times were bad

Acknowledgements

I wish to thank to Kasy, Belinda, and Qudrat, people from three different generations and cultural backgrounds, for reading the manuscript and commenting on it. I am also immensely grateful to Paul Komesaroff and Leigh Rich of Palaver Books for selecting *Asylum* for publication and doing a very professional job with all aspects of its production. My thanks also go to Benjamin Jacob for his evocative cover design.

Channa Wickremesekera

March 2015

ASYLUM

If one amongst the pagans asks thee for asylum grant it to him so that he may hear the word of Allah; and then escort him to where he can be secure. That is because they are men without knowledge.

The Holy Koran

Chapter 9, Verse 6

"KHALID!"

Mum calls. From the kitchen. She is always calling. From the kitchen. "Khalid, eat this!" "Khalid, drink this!" "Khalid, bring your plate here! Don't think I am going to walk all over the house looking for your plate!" And it's always Khalid, never Aisha. I swear if Aisha weren't a girl, she would have been calling her constantly, too. And they say Muslims oppress women.

"Khalid!" She is calling again, and in Dari mind you. Mum has been in Melbourne ten years now, two years less than Dad who first came to Australia all on his own. I have never heard her speak English. Well, except this one time when we went to this pharmacy to get some ointment for a rash Aisha was having. Mum was at the counter, carrying Aisha who didn't have to be carried in the first place. She was old enough to walk, especially the few hundred metres to the pharmacy. But Mum still carried her, the big baby. I am sure if Aisha were not almost as tall as me, Mum would be still carrying her. That's how privileged I reckon she is. But to come back to the story, Mum gives the prescription to the woman at the counter, and this rude bitch shows it to her colleague standing next to her and says loudly, "No wonder they get rashes when covered in that thing."

"That thing," of course, is the cloak Mum's wearing and the *niqab* over her mouth. She didn't even care if we heard. And the other cow giggles like her friend has just tickled her bum or something. They didn't think Mum understood; stupid Muslim woman deprived of freedom and education, they must have thought. But Mum was so angry she told her what she thought, which was not much but quite shocking to the two girls.

"If you rude like that," she hissed in English, "I give you real rash, you silly girl!" The two girls looked as if they had just been kicked by a woman they had thought was a cow. That's when I knew Mum could speak English. It was not very good English, I admit, but good enough to put two rude girls in their place. We had no problems with the prescription after that, even though that was the last time we went anywhere near that pharmacy.

When I told Dad, he laughed and said, "Your mother's English is better than mine," which is not true. Dad speaks better English than Mum and many of his Afghan friends, even though he speaks with a thick accent. He learnt it in Afghanistan where he worked for the government. When he found there was no government to work for, he migrated as a refugee, bringing Mum and us later. When he worked for the government, he had to speak in English often. That is how he learnt his English. But still he likes to compliment Mum.

But, then, if her English is good enough, why the hell doesn't she speak it? I asked her once, and she asked why should she speak in English to me, Aisha, and Dad, not to mention all the other Afghans she speaks to, in anything other than Dari? "You think I am crazy or something to speak in English to people who understand Dari?" she asked. In Dari, of course.

"Khalid!" she is calling again.

"What is it?" I am in the kitchen now, gazing at the lady of the house, plump behind the counter, covered head to toe, only the hands and face showing, ladling two fried eggs onto a plate already heaped with steaming spicy rice. There is a big glass of milk warming in the microwave.

"Here! Eat this!"

She points to the plate. I grin and sit down, sucking in the smell of the eggs and all the spices. The kitchen is always full of the smell of spices. Actually, you can smell it from the front door, even in the front yard if the door is open. I remember one Saturday morning this old White bloke who was looking for an address knocking on our door when Mum was cooking. Dad opens the door, and this dude inhales deeply and says, "Ah, the aroma of the Orient!" I guess he didn't have a clue what the smell was, but seeing Dad he guessed that we must be from the Orient. But that's what people are like, I guess. I have heard people saying some drink tastes like piss. Like they taste piss all the time!

Mum looks at me sniffing at the eggs and the rice and frowns. She knows I like to do this before

I eat because it smells so good, but she also likes to frown when I do so.

"Don't sit there smelling your food. Eat!"

She sounds annoyed, but she is not. She often sounds annoyed. Must be all the work she has been doing since she was a child. She was the eldest of four daughters, and she was baby-sitting since she was five and cooking since she was eight, as her mum was always sick before dying fairly young. Now she doesn't have to look after the sisters, who have children of their own, but she still has to cook. Dad likes to cook, too, but Mum doesn't let him. "Mind your own business," she says, which simply means any business other than cooking. But it keeps her very busy, because she cooks all the time or does something that has something to do with cooking. Gives you little time to think of anything other than the next job, I guess. When she is frying the eggs, she is thinking about warming the milk. When she has warmed the milk, she is thinking about washing the plates. When she is washing the plates, she is thinking about cooking lunch.

"Aisha!" I yell, looking up. The spoilt little brat must be still showering. It's seven twenty already, and she is still showering. The bus will be here in ten minutes, and we will miss it at this rate. She has another thing coming if she thinks I am going to wait for her.

"Why are you yelling?" Mum asks as she takes the milk out. "She will come down soon. She knows where the food is." She puts the milk before me.

"Drink!"

I grin again. I want to say that I, too, know where the food is and she doesn't have to yell. But that doesn't work. A long time ago, Mum decided she was going to yell at me and not at Aisha. Who am I to change tradition? Besides, what is a bit of yelling when you can eat food this good?

"Can I have some more rice?"

Mum looks at me as if I were the cause of all the famines in the world, before taking my plate to heap another mound of rice. "You eat too much!" she says, as she pushes the plate at me. "Do you want another egg?"

"No," I say. "I am trying to cut down." I can see Mum wants to laugh, but she only allows herself a little smile. Busy.

Aisha walks in, fixing her *hijab*. "Why are you

yelling like I am down the road or something?" She frowns and picks up her plate, letting the *hijab* just hang loose over her head.

"If you don't hurry, we will miss the bus" is all I say. But Mum wants her to fix her *hijab* first. "Fix your *hijab* before you eat," she says. "How many times do I have to tell you?"

Aisha starts fixing the scarf. "We have never missed the bus because I am late," she says, still pretending to be grumpy. I smile to myself. She is right. We have only missed the bus when I have slept in. Or when the bus was late—or early. We go to this Muslim school that sends its school buses around in the morning to pick up the kids. The bloke who drives our bus is a grumpy old man who expects us to be at the pick-up point when he arrives, even if it is ten minutes early or ten minutes late. How are we to know what time he is arriving on a particular day? I guess you will have to call him on his mobile, but what is the point in calling somebody who almost never speaks? Fortunately, he is usually late rather than early.

But I don't admit Aisha is right. That would spoil the fun of having a little argument with the little sister. What is the point of having a younger sister if you can't tease her? I remember when I was younger I was having fights with Aisha so often I used to ask Mum and Dad why we couldn't get a brother instead of a sister. And all that Dad did was look up like he was looking for a sign from heaven and say it was Allah's wish. "Then why can't we have a brother at least now," I used to ask, and Dad said it is also Allah's wish that we have no more children. I believed it then, but now I am sure that although the first one may have been Allah's wish and only Allah's wish, the second one was certainly my parents' wish as well. I guess having the two of us is more than enough for them. As for me, I would still be happy to have a brother, but in addition to Aisha, not instead. She is too much fun to tease, the little shit.

"Bloody bastard! Bloody bastard!"

Dad is on the phone to someone. I am not sure who he is speaking to, though. He calls a lot of people "bastard" and not always because he is angry. It's just a word he likes. Almost the only swearing he ever does. Good Australian word, he says. Covers everything and everybody. Any time.

"Who is he yelling at?" Aisha asks, in English, looking at Mum.

"The meat must be late again," Mum says in Dari, setting a plate of rice before Aisha. She knows exactly who Dad is yelling at by listening to the tone of his voice. I guess when you are married to someone for eighteen years you get to know all the tones. Now she knows that the bastard he is yelling at is Frank, who is the bloke who supplies meat to Dad's butcher shop. Dad runs a *halal* butcher shop not far from where we live. He says it's better than working for the government in Afghanistan. "There I worked for butchers, and here I am my own butcher," he says and laughs at his own joke. He can be weird like that sometimes.

Will Nadia get to know my tones like Mum knows Dad's, I wonder as I drink the tea Mum has given me. Nadia is this Lebo chick at our school. Hot, even with the *hijab* on. Hell, she can be in full *burka* and I will find her hot. Curves like that you can't hide with a robe. And she doesn't wear the *hijab* outside and, man, then she can cause an explosion just by being there, killing anyone within a hundred metres with a heatstroke. Of course, not many people know I have the hots for her. Some friends at school do, and Aisha knows, too, I guess, being in the same school. Nadia, I am told, knows it, too, although she acts as if she couldn't care less, which only drives me nuts even more. Mum has no idea, though. She would freak out if she knew I have the hots for a Lebanese girl. She wants me to marry an Afghan so that she can keep talking Dari all her life. Aisha threatens to tell her now and then, but she doesn't. She knows if she does I will tell Mum about Javed, who although he is Afghan is also a prick who smokes like a chimney. Aisha thinks he is hot. I don't really like him, but I guess knowing that Aisha has a thing for him is good insurance. Besides, I don't think Aisha means anything serious with him. Imagine spending the rest of your life cleaning ashtrays! She is not that dumb.

Dad walks in, looking very upset. "The meat is late," he says, sitting at the table. "That bastard Frank never delivers the meat on time. I think I will kick him and Massoud both out." Massoud is the guy who helps Dad at the butcher shop. Nice bloke but a bit thick. For that reason Dad never calls him a bastard. He calls him a donkey. Not all the time but only when he makes a mistake, which is quite often.

He starts eating, threatening Massoud and

Frank with banishment from his business. We all know he is bluffing, though. He has been threatening to kick Frank and Massoud out for the last five years, but he never does. He never says so, but I know Dad thinks that if he kicks out Frank when he has a disabled wife and four children to feed, Allah will do something worse to him, like making sure the meat is never there on time, no matter whom he hires, bastard or not. Massoud is another piece of work. Fourteen children. Dad will keep him, too. Doesn't want Allah to send twelve more kids like us, I guess. I don't think he wants him or Mum to go through that. Children are a treasure, I have heard Dad say to people. But I am sure there are some treasures you don't want to have too much of.

He pauses and looks at the lawn outside. The grass is getting long even if it's the middle of winter. "Did Mustafa bring back the lawnmower?" he asks in Dari so Mum replies.

"No," she says. "Not yet."

"Bloody bastard!" Dad says again before he returns to his food. That was definitely meant for Mustafa. Even I can see that. Mustafa, or Uncle Mustafa as we sometimes call him, is this old

Afghan dude who lives down the street, in the last house next to the little playground. He lives with his wife and four sons and does little work other than walking up and down the road and chatting to anybody and anything that moves, thanks to Centrelink. He is a nice bloke, but he irritates Dad because he comes round to borrow the lawnmower all the time, even in the middle of winter. His lawn must be the best kept lawn on the street, courtesy of our mower into which he has never poured even a spoonful of petrol. But Dad always lets him have it, as he has been living on welfare even though he is fit enough to work, and Dad calls him a bloody bastard for it. Besides, Mustafa is also a kind man. If he had any petrol left he would mow Little Barry's lawn as well, for the sake of charity. Little Barry, the little Aussie bloke who used to live in the house opposite to Mustafa's, never had any time for mowing his lawn or doing anything else because he was always drinking. Mum said he must be lonely or sad or something, because he just drank, never hurt anybody. Actually he drank himself to death only two weeks ago, a day after Mustafa had done a great job on his lawn—with our petrol.

"Turn the TV on," Dad says, looking up from the plate. He likes to watch TV when he is having breakfast and dinner. And our TV is now placed so strategically that you can watch it from the kitchen table. Dad chose the spot for it and was very proud of it. He is always shifting and moving things in the house when he is free. It's like a hobby, I guess. His name is Rustum, and some of the Aussie customers who have been buying lamb and beef from him for years call him Rusty. But there is nothing rusty about my Dad. The number of times our furniture has been moved around is proof of that. He calls it the "Movement of the Furnitures." I know it sounds like some seasonal migration of birds or something, but the only thing the seasonal migration of birds has in common with the Movement of the Furnitures is the movement. The birds move seasonally, but the "furnitures" move almost weekly. They are always on the move, our furniture. It is a bit hard to keep up with the movements sometimes, because what used to be the sofa last week could suddenly turn out to be the dining table today. But the TV will stay for a while, I guess. That spot was a real discovery for Dad. "I should have been an interior designer," he kept saying for several days after that, because he could now watch the news and current affairs while having his breakfast and dinner at the kitchen table and having little chats with Mum. Mum doesn't mind all the movements as long as things in the kitchen remain where they are.

Mum turns the TV on using the remote that she keeps in the kitchen. I think she is very grateful for Dad's interior designing skills, as now she can turn the TV on from the kitchen and keep it on while cooking, watching it now and then when she needs a break. She doesn't care what she watches as long as there is nothing rude. Fat chance of that happening between morning and evening!

The TV comes to life. That reminds me. Wonder who won the footy last night, the Blues or the Hawks? For some reason they were playing the game on a Thursday evening, and I had no time to watch it because I had some stupid assignment to finish. Mum said I should finish the homework and then watch TV. It was so late when I finished I just went to bed without even checking the scores.

There is a newsbreak on. The Prime Minister

is saying something, or trying to say something, but we don't get it, as usual. I think prime ministers are meant to be like that. I have heard several prime ministers and premiers speaking on TV for the last ten years but never understood what they were saying. I guess it's a politician thing. I remember once this local MP dude came to our mall during one election and went around shaking hands and talking to people, especially to little children. I did not understand a word he was saying, even though I listened carefully because he looked so keen. He even said *as-salaam alaikum* to Dad while trying hard not to stare at Mum wearing the *niqab*. Then he went on to say something about how badly misunderstood Muslims are, and we just stood there smiling and nodding our heads like idiots, wondering if he realized how badly he was understood by us.

"Bloody bastard," says Dad again, and we are not sure if he still means Frank or Mustafa or now he has decided to bastardize the PM. No matter. The volume is gradually fading. A sure sign his anger is dying.

A woman has given birth to triplets, for the second time, according to the newswoman. A woman after Massoud's heart, I guess. Three for the price of one.

"*Hamdulillah!*" says Mum, looking at the woman on the screen looking so happy with her three little babies dressed in identical baby clothes. She probably thinks it's a miracle, but a miracle she can surely do without. Imagine cooking for that lot! Somebody has broken out of a juvenile detention centre, the newsreader is saying now. A seventeen-year-old kid. He has shot a guard and is on the run with a gun. Supposed to be dangerous. I reckon! If he has shot a guard and is carrying a gun, he has to be.

"Bloody bastard." Now the tone is very low. The anger is subsiding.

"What is a juvenile detention centre?" Aisha asks.

God! What ignorance! And she is already fifteen.

"That's where you are heading," I can't help saying. I grin at my own smart crack. But Aisha ignores me. She has her own comeback.

"He looks hot!" she says without even looking at me.

I look at the screen. There is the picture of a

boy, with dirty blond hair, kind of skinny and malnourished, face full of freckles. Hot? If that is hot, most guys in the world must be sizzling.

"You obviously don't know hot from cold," I say like an adult putting down a smartass kid. "But good match. Former detainee marrying future detainee."

"That's enough!" Mum snaps, picking up our plates. Aisha looks at me and sticks her tongue out as if to say you may have your wit but I have Mum. I can't help but smile at her cheek. Wouldn't have it any other way. Mum knows that, too.

Dad is eating silently now. No more bastardizing.

"What happened to the footy?" I ask, looking at no one in particular. The newsbreak had ended without a word on the game.

"Carlton won," answers Dad. But I am not sure. Dad is far better at telling his lamb from his beef than knowing Carlton from Manchester United. How many times have I heard him telling people this or that team had won the footy when that team wasn't even playing? He just likes to give an opinion on something, all the time. Well, not really. Only when Mum doesn't have one.

No matter, I will check at school. School is full of people who know which team plays which.

"Let's go," I say, picking up my bag.

Aisha looks at me as if there were another hour for the bus. But she gets up anyway.

"Bye, Mum, bye, Dad," we say as we walk to the front door. All that Mum says is to hurry up before we miss the bus. Dad only raises his hand to show that our departure has registered with him. He may not be bastardizing Frank any more, but I can see that he is still thinking of the meat.

I open the door, but we can't get out.

There is someone standing there. A boy, tall, dirty blond hair, the face skinny, kind of malnourished, lots of freckles.

And in his hand, a gun.

2 "I THOUGHT YOU WERE GOING," I hear Dad say behind me as we back up into the house. That is exactly what we thought, too, but we found this nutter standing outside, with a gun, blocking our path. Now here we are backing up into the house like we have seen a ghost.

The delinquent follows us in. And I am sure it is the delinquent. Who else could it be with those freckles and that gun? A Jehovah's Witness? But I wish the TV woman had been more specific about which direction he had run away. Then we would have at least been a little bit more prepared for this sudden visit. Now all we can do is let him walk in.

And he is coming in, stepping cautiously like he is not sure where he is going, stealing glances over his shoulder as if he is expecting to be ambushed from behind at any moment. He is holding the gun up now, pointing it at us, but I can see the hands shaking slightly. I also notice that his face is really freckled, like he has some skin condition that has left his face full of red spots. The eyes are pale, trying to look mean, and the dark blond hair dancing on his head. And as he enters the house, he is hit by the smell of the food. He sniffs at the air a bit, uncertainly, as if smelling something for the first time. But I don't expect him to say, "Ah, the smell of the Orient." He wouldn't know the Orient from his prison cell, I guess. Come to think of it, I myself didn't know what it was. I thought it was a planet or star or something until our English teacher told me it is not. But I don't think any teacher would want to go anywhere near this dude to explain anything. Not with that attitude and that gun.

He keeps edging us into the house, and as he does so, he shuts the door behind him with his foot. Doesn't want anyone outside to see. Whatever he is going to do he wants to do behind closed doors; understandable if you are running away from prison, but I am a bit worried about what he has in mind.

The gun itself is not too bad. An ordinary handgun. I have seen bigger guns than that in Afghanistan with kids half his size. And they carry them with a lot more confidence than this dude whose hands are shaking. But I have never had a gun pointed at me, big or small. And the shaking hands are not helping things, either. I glance sideways at Aisha, and she is staring at the gun, eyes as big as little saucers.

The delinquent sees our worried look and realizes he is not the only nervous one there. He gets bold.

"Get in!" he barks, pointing to the lounge behind us, and then tells us, "Move!"

I guess he must have learnt all this ordering in prison. They probably do a lot of barking and ordering about there. I have seen this in movies. He may have even seen them in movies in prison. Delinquent see, delinquent do.

And now he is also realizing that we are different. I am pretty fair, but anyone can see I am not White. And Aisha, well, the *hijab* says it all.

But he doesn't realize how different we are until he sees Mum.

"What is wrong with you? Why aren't you going?" she says coming out of the kitchen. "The bus must have gone now. Who is that shouting?"

You can feel the distress in her voice, but it's nowhere close to ours. But we are not game to tell her that we can't leave because there is an idiot pointing a gun at us.

Then she sees the idiot and freezes. "*Hamdulillah*!" That's the first thing she says. And the first thing she does? Pulls her *niqab* right over her mouth.

I can never get over this. My mother would rather die than expose her full face to a strange male. She's got to be one of the few Afghan women who do this in Australia but, boy, she does it with a passion! I have seen her laughing and chatting to women with just the *hijab* on, and along comes a man she has never seen and she is pulling up the scarf like he's got a disease. "There is nothing wrong with showing your face," I have heard Dad say a million times. "This is Australia, and your face is very pretty." And Mum always says, "Allah is Allah everywhere. Australia or Afghanistan. And it is enough if you see my face." And they say Muslim men oppress their women!

And now, too, she is covering her face, quickly, rapidly, as if she is afraid the kid has already seen too much.

But it freaks him out. I bet he has never seen a woman so up close with her face covered. Come to think of it, I don't think he has ever seen a Muslim—except on TV where they are mostly terrorists or terrorist suspects, blowing up things or planning to blow up things. Enough to make anyone worried without ever seeing a Muslim.

And so he freaks out. Big time. "What the fuck!" he yells as if he had seen a ghost. "What the fuck! What are you doing? What is that shit? Take it off!" he cries. I am sure it is very unsettling to him. Well, I guess it is unsettling to anybody if you are not used to it. I can still remember the look on that MP dude's face when he met Mum at the mall during the election campaign. He was trying hard not to look at her straight, but you could tell he was nervous. And that was an MP who probably meets more freaks than most people. It must really freak out a kid who has never seen a Muslim.

And he is going spastic. Truly. "Take it off!" he yells. "Take the fucking thing off!"

We stand frozen. Now Dad is there, too, standing next to Mum. I am sure they both realize by now who has walked in. I can see it in Mum's eyes, and Dad's got his mouth wide open, like he is competing with the delinquent in the freak-out stakes. Actually, I am not sure if it's Dad or the delinquent who is more freaked out.

And I am scared, truly scared. The kid is pointing the gun at Mum, yelling her to drop the *niqab*. He is steadily going spastic, ballistic even. And the hands are shaking even harder now.

I reach out and hold Aisha's hand. Hell! It's cold. Just like mine. I look at Dad, and he has gone stiff, too. Everything frozen solid. Lips so tight they cannot utter a word. Not even bloody bastard.

But not Mum. To all those people who think Muslim women are meek and timid, come to my home. I will show you a Muslim woman who knows no fear. My Mum! She shakes her head to show that she is not budging, that the boy will have to take the scarf off only when she is fully dead. And she says it. "Over my dead body," she says. "Only over my dead body you will make me take my scarf off and expose my face to your unruly eyes," she says, loudly and clearly. There is only one little problem. She says it in Dari.

The boy is confused. Not only is he seeing a woman covered almost head to toe, but she is also having a go at him in a foreign language. What sort of country he has fled to, he must be wondering. And the hands are shaking harder now. Fuck! I am thinking. Don't let it go off, God please don't let it go off, my Mum is my life. Don't let it go off. I will fast six months a year and pray fifty times a day, don't let it go off! And sorry for swearing.

I can feel in Aisha's hand that she is thinking the same.

Now Dad gets bolder. He steps in front of Mum, shielding her. "Don't you threaten her!" he says to the boy in English. He has found his voice. Well, only a little bit of it, as it sounds really faint. "Don't you threaten her, you bloody bastard!" he croaks, standing right in front of Mum.

Good on ya, Dad! Brilliant thinking! Stand there right in front and call him a bastard, and if the bastard lets the bloody thing off, you can go to heaven with Mum. Don't mind us poor orphans.

Now Mum pushes Dad aside and stands in

front of him, still speaking in Dari. This is like a crazy competition to see who can get shot first. And she is still yelling at him. But now she is not telling the boy why she is not taking the scarf off. She is telling him off! Yes, she is telling him off for shooting people and going around threatening people.

"Are you out of your mind?" she is asking. "Is this what you are doing with the life God has given you? Shooting people and breaking into people's homes? Threatening them? You should be ashamed of yourself!"

The kid is totally confused now. What sort of people are these, he must be wondering. And what a woman! Yelling at me like this. And I am the one with the gun!

But you can also see that he has sensed that Mum is now saying something different, that she is not speaking about the scarf but about him. I guess he would have had a mother, too, at some stage, before he decided to go off and become a delinquent. Or maybe he didn't. A proper mother, I mean. That's probably why he is a delinquent.

But he is not giving up, either. I guess he realizes that Mum is getting the upper hand, that her yelling is making him nervous, but he doesn't know what to do. They didn't prepare him for this in prison.

So he just stands there, pointing the gun at her. But his whole body is shaking, his eyes darting from my Mum to my Dad and then from them to us.

"Shut up!" he cries. "Shut the fuck up!" The swearing only makes my Mum worse. Her pitch rises.

"Silly boy!" she yells. "Don't you swear at me, you silly boy!"

I am suddenly feeling a bit relaxed now, maybe because I see that the delinquent is quite shaken. Relaxed enough to be a smartass.

"He doesn't speak Dari," I tell Mum in Dari. "Why can't you speak English at least at a time like this?"

Mum scowls at me. "Don't tell me what to do!" she hisses in Dari. "I will speak whatever I want."

I shrug my shoulders. I hope Nadia is not this stubborn. I don't want to spend the rest of my life trying to fix one little problem. Provided my Mum lets me marry her, of course.

"Shut up!" the kid shouts again. He is getting

really spastic now, seeing us having our little conversation, leaving him to hold the gun. But I continue to relax. It is as if somehow I know that the delinquent is not that dangerous. Time for another smart remark.

"This, my sister, is a delinquent," I say to Aisha, squeezing her hand. Big brother furthering the education of the sister. But that only makes the delinquent really angry. His face goes totally red; the freckles glow as he looks at me with eyes that can kill.

"One more word outta you, and I'll blow your brains out." I am sure he picked up the lines from a movie. They watch a lot of movies in prison. You watch enough crime movies, you will talk like a criminal or a cop, my English teacher says. Here is living proof, I guess.

"Sorry," I say. "Couldn't help it." Of course, he is bluffing. That was more than one word, and my brains are still inside my head. I can't help smirking. "You still think he is hot?" I ask my sister, in Dari though. The delinquent may be bluffing, but I don't want to push my luck. I still need my brains. I can hear Aisha giggling behind me. Good to see she is relaxed, too.

But now it's Mum who has a go at me. "Keep quiet!" she orders. "Don't make him angry."

I am making him angry? What about her going off at him! Well, I know better not to argue. I shut up, giving the delinquent a smug look to say that my Mum is more powerful than your gun.

And the kid seems exhausted now. I guess he was before he came in. He must have been on the run the whole night. Probably hungry, too. Now on top of all that he has to put up with a family of very strange people.

"All of you shut the fuck up!" he yells. "Shut up!"

He waves the gun at us. He seems to be so very close to losing it. I only hope he doesn't squeeze the trigger when he does. But suddenly he is distracted, his eyes drawn to the TV. Why shouldn't they be? There is another newsbreak, and he is there. Again. Freckled face plastered on the screen. The police are searching for him, the newsreader says. And they are closing in on him. Fast.

The next thing we know, the TV screen is gone. Blasted. The kid must have really lost it hearing that the cops were closing in on him. Or he was just really pissed off, with the cops, with us, with everybody. Whatever it is, he points the gun at the screen and bang! The two-thousand-dollar flat-screen TV explodes into a hundred pieces, along with the freckled face on it.

And he doesn't stop at shooting the TV. He starts shooting at random, like a maniac. At the wall, at the sofa, even at the computer monitor in the corner. Boom! Boom! All gone.

I hit the ground the moment I realize what the nutter is about to do. As I do, I look at Mum to see if she is hitting the ground. She is, but that is because Dad is pushing her and landing on top of her to protect her. I look at Aisha, and she is under the dining table, her hands on her ears.

It is scary. The idiot is going crazy. But it is also comforting in a way to know that he is shooting at everything except us. The kid is no killer. He has a whole family before him to shoot but shoots the stuffing out of the sofa. My brains have nothing to fear.

But he is not done yet. The TV reporter had said that the cops were closing in on him. Now he decides he wants to make sure that they won't. So he grabs the phone and yanks it out of the socket. He takes one look at the fire in the fireplace and, before we can gasp in horror, throws the phone into the flames. Just like that. Then he asks for our mobile phones. He doesn't want any one of us sending any unnecessary text messages giving the game away. Not just a freckled face, our delinquent. No TV, no telephone, no Internet, and no texting, and hopefully nobody will know he is here pointing his little gun at us.

We hand him our mobiles. Even though we are quite convinced he is not likely to shoot us, we still don't want to take any chances. So we hand them over. All four of them. At first there were only three, mine, Dad's, and Aisha's, but then the kid looks at Mum as if asking, "Where is yours?" I didn't think he'd expected her to have one, too, but I guess by now he has realized she is capable of anything. I am surprised he didn't think she was hiding another computer inside her robe.

But Mum hands him her mobile. I thought she might refuse, but she doesn't. We soon realize why. The battery's gone, she explains to Dad in Dari as she hands over her phone. She was going to get it charged this morning but then the delinquent had walked in.

Having gathered all the communication devices, the delinquent throws them into the fire. Casually, like he is only adding more fuel to the fire, not sending Dad's three-hundred-dollar Nokia or my sixty-dollar Samsung all up in smoke. They make a spluttering noise among the flames, like they are bursting or something.

The kid is getting a bit pumped now. Probably because he is satisfied that now he is safe. And all that shooting had got the adrenalin rushing. He celebrates it by shooting into the fire, pointing the gun like you see them do in movies. Bang!

But he can't.

There is no bang, only a little click. He has run out of ammo. The idiot has shot all the bullets in that frenzy of shooting. He wasn't so bright, after all. I should have known, if I had bothered counting the shots. But who has the time to count shots when all you think of is dodging them? Besides, I am not very good at counting anyway.

But it's a relief to know that the gun is empty, that if he still wants to blow our brains out, he can't.

And now suddenly the tables are turned. Now he is just a kid, with an empty gun, against four of us, and one of them a feisty woman who was not scared even when the gun had bullets.

He knows he's had it. He watches us gathering ourselves from the floor, like the dead coming to life, almost in slow motion, and as he watches his face shows all the signs that he knows he is well and truly fucked. He is mostly concerned about Mum. He looks at her as if expecting her to grab him and throw him into the fire very soon.

But it's Dad who strikes. I guess he had been waiting to do this ever since the kid walked in, but the bullets prevented him. Now he snatches the gun from the kid and throws it to me. Then, he smacks the kid across the face.

"Bloody bastard!" he says loudly. I am sure he was waiting to say that, too. Loudly and freely. "Bloody bastard!" he cries again as he hits the kid again and again.

The delinquent is helpless. He was already demoralized when he realized he had shot all the bullets. But now he is completely beaten. He doesn't even try to hit back. He just holds up his arms to defend himself like any helpless kid would. But that does nothing to stop Dad. He just smacks him and smacks him as if he were in a fit. This is the first time I have seen Dad hit anyone. His violence is usually verbal and that, too, mostly limited to "bloody bastard." But now he is truly going nuts with the smacking! He starts by slapping him front- and backhand, again and again, and then begins to mix in a punch or two. Take that and that and that, too, for coming into our house and threatening us and destroying our property, he seems to be saying with each slap and punch. The kid can only put up his hands to protect himself, not a very good defence against an angry Afghan.

I got to admit I don't mind it at first; the little prick deserves it, for all the shit he's put us through. But now I am also getting a bit worried. Dad is getting a little bit carried away, even though many of the smacks and punches are landing on those bony arms. At this rate, I expect him to throw in a few kicks any moment and that would be a bit scary. What if Dad really hurts him before we call the cops? I don't want any more trouble than we already have.

Fortunately Mum intervenes. "Enough!" she cries, pulling at his arm. "Enough! You will kill him!" Dad looks at her as if to say that that is exactly what he intends to do. But the look in my mother's eyes stops him. My mother often says there is no need for a woman to show any part of her body as long as her eyes are visible. I never realized what she meant until this moment. Man! If looks could kill!

Dad stops the assault and sits down on the sofa, panting. The kid slumps on the sofa opposite Dad, the sofa he has just shot up. He is crying now. Not a delinquent any more. Just a kid.

Skinny, freckled, and now full of tears.

"Get me some water," Dad says. Aisha goes to the kitchen to get some water. All that smacking has made Dad thirsty. And he keeps panting, staring at the delinquent as if only taking a short break before another assault. The delinquent is not game to look at him, probably because he is expecting more punches and slaps. He sits like a sack of bones, sobbing, and his bony body shaking like he's got some terrible fit or something. Judging by the state he is in, he seems to be in need of water, too. "What about him?" I ask Dad as Aisha returns with a big glass of water. I don't want the idiot to pass out before we hand him to the cops.

"Yes, give some to him, too," Mum says from the kitchen. She has gone back to the kitchen. It's as if that were her home. The delinquent walks in, threatens us, then she comes out of the kitchen, gives him an earful, and after he has been neutralized, goes back to the kitchen. I am surprised she doesn't sleep there.

Aisha brings another glass of water, and I give it to the kid. He does nothing at first, but then when he realizes that the glass is not going to go away unless he takes it, he grabs it. He puts it to his mouth and starts drinking as if he had not had a drop of water for a week.

He drains the glass. I can hear Aisha giggle somewhere behind me.

I frown at her. Don't want little sister getting too relaxed about the freckle-boy. I haven't forgotten that she had thought he was hot.

"Get the tissues," I tell her in Dari, and she brings the tissue box. The idiot is sniffling, and his snot is all over his shirt. I don't want it all over the sofa, too. He has already spoilt it enough by shooting it up. I give him the tissues, and he takes one. What a dumbass! Like that is going to be enough! There is enough snot there to fill a bucket, and he takes one! I keep holding the box until he takes more. Then he blows his nose like he is going to bring all that water out, through the nose.

Mum comes out with a brush and a dust pan. She wants to clean up the debris. She sees the delinquent has finished the water and shakes her head. "Want some more?" Mum asks in Dari. I translate. The kid says nothing. He just looks at us blankly. I guess he wants more but feels embarrassed or too scared to ask. Mum takes the empty glass away and brings in another glass filled to the brim.

As he begins to drink, Mum squats and begins to clean up his mess.

"Why are you doing that?" Dad asks her. "Get the bastard to clean it up." Too right, I think. He makes the mess, and he should clean it up before we hand him to the coppers.

But Mum frowns at Dad and says this is her house and she will clean it. If we want, we can help. Then I go to her to help, and she shoos me away.

"Mind your own business," she says and then tells me what business to mind. "Keep an eye on the boy."

I look at the delinquent. He is drinking the second glass of water, and as he drinks his eyes roll all around, looking at all of us, Mum on the floor, me in front of him, Dad on the sofa, and even Aisha, who has gone back to the table under which she was hiding when he was shooting like a lunatic. He seems scared and uncertain. Must be wondering what we are going to do to him. Strange creatures from another planet feeding me water before they consume me, he probably thinks.

But it doesn't stop him from drinking. While the eyes roll, the water disappears, fast.

He has almost finished it when we hear the noise. The chopper, right above us. And then the sirens.

THE COPS MUST HAVE BEEN in the area for a while. They don't suddenly home in on a place like that unless they know where to look or unless they have been alerted by something or somebody. The kid must have seen them before he decided to barge into our house; that is why he was looking over his shoulder all the time, I suddenly realize. I don't think anybody knew where he was until he started shooting like an idiot. The cops probably had a tip-off that he had been seen in the area, and they must have been prowling around when the shots rang out.

But now they are here. In full force. I look out the window, through the blinds, and all I see are cops. Everywhere. There are at least three cop cars in the street, and there are heaps of cops behind the cars. Our house has this low wall at the front, about knee-high. There are cops behind that, too, crouching, like they are expecting to be shot at any moment. Some of them are even wearing their bullet-proof jackets! We can't see what's happening on either side of our garden because there are thick hedges there, but I am sure there are cops along the fence in the neighbours' gardens, hiding behind those bushes. Aisha looks out the back window and confirms there are cops behind the back fence, too. And as if it's not enough, there is also the big-ass helicopter above us, surely filled with cops. I really don't know why the police always say they don't have enough coppers to fight crime. There must be at least fifty of them here, all to catch a scared kid with a handgun. If only they knew that the delinquent is already defeated and in tears!

I look at Dad and Mum. I don't have to tell them. We are surrounded. They know it.

And the kid knows it, too. Suddenly he looks scared shitless. I guess he was when he walked in, just that he hid it well. But now there is nothing to hide it with. The bullets are gone and so is the gun. What's he going to hide his fear with? His freckles?

He is looking at us like we are going to kill him or something, and the eyes look as if they are pleading, but the lips are either too scared—or proud—to move.

Dad looks at him. A thin smile on his lips. "I think your time has come, boy!"

I swear my Dad should have been a movie star. In a gangster movie. He is so good at making those tough gangster comments. I think your time has come, boy! I remember once when we were visiting Afghanistan and attending a cousin's wedding these dudes were firing rifles in the air. They always fire rifles there, wedding or no wedding. And at this wedding, they were firing lots of them, even kids. Dad took one of the guns and gave it to the brother of the guy who was getting married, a sixteen-year-old kid, and said in English, "Come on, tough guy, show us what you got!" The kid and most of the people who were there had no idea what he was saying, but Aisha and I just cracked up.

And now this, I think your time has come, boy!

True, he sounds like a gangster only when he talks like that, which is not often. Most times he is pretty normal. But then the kid doesn't know it, does he? All he can see is that the guy who beat him up only a few minutes ago is talking tough and is threatening to throw him to the cops outside. His lips begin to quiver as if to show that he is not liking it. He is too scared to say it.

"Guess you better get ready, boy!" Another tough statement. But I can see Dad is not sure of the tone any more. It's getting slightly soft. I am not sure if it is because Mum is looking at him really sternly or because the kid has gone completely white.

He started going white as soon as we took the gun from him, but then Dad's smacking brought the blood back to his veins, though fortunately not out of them. I guess he went back to turning white soon after Mum intervened and saved him, and the process kind of accelerated when the chopper appeared with the carloads of cops outside. Now it had completed, and he was white. You know how people say somebody is as white as a sheet? I always thought they exaggerated—until today. Until I saw the kid go white. He was white.

Whiter than a sheet. Those freckles all gone; fear was like some magical formula for freckles. All gone, leaving him whiter than a sheet.

And from where she stood, Mum had seen it all, and she was not taking kindly to Dad playing tough guy. You could see it in her eyes. You can't scare him any more than this was what she was trying to say, I guess. Hell, you couldn't scare anybody any more than that!

But I am not ready to go soft on him. "Shall I call them in?" I ask Dad, looking at Mum. I guess I can be really mean sometimes, but then what do you expect after all that the idiot has done? Flat-screen TV, computer, phones, all gone in seconds, not to mention threatening us with his stupid gun. Do we want him here any more? But Dad looks at Mum. Mum looks back at him. There is some profound eye communication going on that I cannot understand. I think I am a pretty good judge of Mum's eye language, but there are certain words and phrases that only a husband can understand. She was telling him something, and he was listening, as Dad always does when Mum has that kind of look. He wasn't saying anything.

Then Mum says it in words. I guess she wanted

us to know as well. "We can't hand him in," she says. "It's not right."

I look at Mum in disbelief. Is she crazy? I mean, the little prick comes into our house, holds us at gunpoint, threatens her, and shoots up our TV, computer, and sofa and throws our mobiles in the fire, and she thinks we shouldn't hand him over!

But it's Aisha who puts it into words.

"Are you crazy?" she asks in Dari. "After all he has done?" But Mum is unmoved. It takes a lot more than an indignant son and daughter to move her. Like a cowering, beaten kid, for instance.

"Look at him," she says. "He is helpless. We can't hand him to the police. He depends on us."

I look at the delinquent. He sits there, huddled on the sofa he shot up just ten minutes ago, visibly shaking as if expecting some thundering blow to land on him any time or something like that. His eyes are glued to the carpet, not game enough to look at us. All the pretensions are fast disappearing, and I can see tears reappearing in his eyes. Yes, he is helpless; scared shitless is more like it. But that is because he has lost his gun. If he had his gun, with bullets, he would have been still barking at us. At Mum.

But all that matters to Mum is that he is help-less now.

I look at Dad. I know there is no point in look-ing at Dad when Mum has made her decision, but I wonder how he really feels. Sometimes Dad agrees with Mum because he agrees, but other times because there is no point in disagreeing. I want to know which one it is now.

And I can see that Dad is like half—half in a half-hearted way. A bit of agreement here, a bit of disagreement there, but overall no serious contest.

"The boy is at our mercy now," Mum is saying. "We can't give him to the cops. It is not our way. Not the Afghan way, not the Islamic way."

Oh, I have heard all this before! How you should look after people who take refuge with you, even if they are your worst enemies. Even if they have killed your own mother and father. I always thought that sort of thing happened only a long time ago, and if it happened now, it was only in movies. Never thought we will have to practise it.

"Do we have to take it so seriously?" I ask. I mean it. This is the twenty-first century. Internet,

Facebook, iPods. Do we have to go back to tribal days? I look at Dad, and he seems to agree, at least halfway, even though he doesn't say it. He has a Facebook page. Not much activity going on there; just a few friends, including me and Aisha. But he has made it to the Internet. Mum would, too, I guess, if she ever gets out of the kitchen.

Mum reads my mind. "The Koran was written when there was no Internet," she says. "You think we should not take it seriously because the Prophet doesn't have a website?"

Maybe not, I think. But I can't help thinking that if the Prophet were alive today, he would at least have a Facebook page. And a cool one, too.

"Well, he didn't exactly come looking for refuge, did he?" Aisha joins in now. Good girl! At time like this I am willing to make allowance for her cheek.

There is only one problem, though. She is trying that on Mum.

"Well, he is not exactly threatening us now, is he?" she asks. "It is we who are holding him prisoner."

Dad looks at me as if the argument has been closed quite convincingly. He doesn't like arguing with Mum because he can't win, especially when religion is involved. Your Mum knows more about Islam than most mullahs, he often says proudly. She learnt it from her dad, who was some respected scholar in Afghanistan. But that doesn't stop Dad from looking at the TV like he is mourning a favourite family member cruelly murdered. Then he looks at the fire and takes a deep breath. Our house is one of the few houses in this part of town with a real fireplace. Dad had it set up especially because he likes the feel of a real fire in the winter. I don't think he ever thought that fire was going to swallow his mobile, thanks to the creature from delinquent-land.

But he doesn't want to argue with Mum. And realizing he can't beat her, he joins her, adding a bit of his own wisdom to Mum's argument. He reminds me what our imam says, all the time trying hard not to look at the TV. The Australian Government may have given you the visa, but Allah has given you your life, the imam thunders often in his *khutbah*. Do what Allah wills.

But I am still not convinced. For one thing, I am certain that the imam wouldn't have taken Allah's word so seriously if his visa was to be withdrawn.

And I am sure there is something somewhere in the Koran we can use for this moment, like one of them precedents I have seen lawyers use on TV. But if I tell my parents that, they will just give me that look that says that I don't know my Koran from my *Law and Order*. I don't like that look. Makes me feel so alone.

So I turn to Aisha for some more encouragement, but the silly girl is staring at the delinquent. Don't tell me she is finding him hot again!

Mum notices it, too.

"Aisha!" she says sternly. "Go to your room!"

Little sister pouts and walks away.

Dad looks at Mum. "You think it's a good idea to leave her alone in the room with cops running around with guns?" Mum sees his point.

"Aisha!" she calls again. "Come here!"

Aisha comes, still pouting. "Why don't you make up your mind?" she asks, but Mum just points to the dining table in the corner. Good thing Dad had moved it to the corner during last week's great Movement of the Furnitures. It was closer to the sofa before that. But then the sofa was also closer to the door last week. Such is the drama caused by the Movement of the Furnitures.

"Sit!" Aisha sits, very hard, to show that she is following orders with the greatest reluctance. But that is good enough for Mum. The table is the place farthest from the delinquent. From there Aisha can still see the kid, but I guess Mum thinks what she sees from there is not as dangerous as what she would have seen from where I am sitting, which is right in front of the creature from freckle-land. And Mum is happy for Aisha not to cover her face. She is that strict only with herself, not with Aisha. I guess she knows it would make Aisha get really moody if she made her do that. She doesn't want her children to be moody. I guess as far as her children are concerned, Mum is willing to bend the rules a bit, hoping, or knowing, that God won't mind. So Aisha just wears the *hijab*.

Suddenly everything has gone quiet. The delinquent sits on the sofa staring at the glass he has just emptied. Now he is occasionally glancing at us, the way kids look at teachers when they have been caught at something, wanting to be brave but too scared to do so. He has no idea what is going on, as we have been discussing things in Dari. But I guess he knows something is going on. We haven't called the police in. Maybe he is guessing his time hasn't come yet.

We sit staring at him, like people who have just realized we have a burden we wish to throw away but can't. Outside the bustle continues, the chopper still circles.

Watching him sitting there with his freckled face and dirty blond hair, I suddenly realize this is the first time we have had an Aussie in our house. Oh, there have been Aussies coming to our house before, like that dude looking for the address, but no one has actually come inside, if you know what I mean. All the others have come looking for something or the other, and they never stepped inside. Even that guy looking for the address left after commenting on the aroma of the Orient and finding out that the number he was looking for was eighty-five, not thirty-five, because whoever the idiot was who wrote the address down for him did not know how to write numbers clearly. We do have Aussie friends but not the kinds who visit homes. Dad knows a few people who are also his customers, and I know a few guys at the local club where I play footy, but they are not close enough for us to visit each other's homes. I generally hang out with other Afghans and a couple of Lebos, but friends of Mum and Dad are almost all Afghans. I guess it's mainly an Islamic thing as well as a cultural thing. But it's also a pity. You got to wait for some crazy kid to barge into your house to have an Aussie in your home. In Australia.

We continue to wait. The wall clock ticks loudly, as if it had suddenly come alive. It's so annoying, I tell you. When everything else is quiet, you can hear it like it's going inside your ear or something. It has always been so. I just wish the delinquent had shot that instead of the TV and the computer.

"That bastard Massoud must be wondering what happened to me," Dad says, his mind suddenly returning to the meat. He gives the delinquent another mean look. "Probably trying to call the mobile." The kid keeps his eyes firmly on the floor. He knows he has sinned. Badly. He has already been soundly beaten for his sins, and he is not sure what further punishments await him.

Mum assures Dad that Massoud will be all right. We must be in the news, she says. On radio and on the Internet. On TV.

The TV! I suddenly realize we must be all over TV! Our house, our street. If we could only watch it. Have they heard of it at school? I am sure they have. This kind of thing gets known very quickly. I am sure my mates, Aisha's mates, and Dad's mates have all tried to call us and text us to find out what's going on. We would have told them, if the delinquent had not thrown the phones into the fire.

I look at the kid with disgust. You come into our house, make us famous, and then take away our opportunity to enjoy it, I want to say. But I don't have to say it. One look at me and the delinquent knows it. He turns his eyes away from mine. He is not game for any more confrontation for the moment, I guess. Or maybe he just wants to hide the tears.

Then there is a noise. A voice, of somebody calling through a loudhailer:

"We know you are in there! Lay down your weapon and come outside with your arms raised. Nothing will happen to you!"

A faint smile passes over the kid's lips. I am sure he has heard that kind of assurance before. Many times, maybe. Dad and Mum look at each other and then at the kid. The kid looks at them. The lips are tight, trying to defy, but the eyes are pleading. And full of tears, too. My parents see the eyes. They look at each other again. Some silent conversation takes place, and then Dad gets up and walks to the door. I can hear him sigh. Deeply. Maybe inside he is still only half agreeing with Mum.

He opens the door a crack and looks out. I, too, get up and part the blinds ever so slightly. There are cops all over the street, and they are all standing behind their cars. I can see some with flak jackets and guns. It would have been so cool if it were somebody else's house.

The cops see Dad peeping. One of them who looks like the boss calls out.

"Is he there?"

Dad says nothing. He just stares at the cop. I look at the kid, and he has gone very white again.

"We want to speak to him."

Dad stands there wondering what to say. I guess he is wondering how to lie without giving it away and without offending God. Dad doesn't like lying. I have never heard him tell a lie or anything I suspect to be a lie. But then I guess he has never been in a situation where he had to lie—until now. That is why he is taking a long time to answer, wondering how he is going to get around this one. But he is taking too long, way too long for the delinquent. I have been looking at him and Dad and have noticed how with each second Dad hesitates, the kid's face gets whiter and tighter as if he were going to burst or something. Then, suddenly, he snaps.

"Fuck off!" he yells. "Fuck off, you pigs, or I will shoot everyone here!"

I can see the cops scurrying behind their cars. The boss cop first. Pretty brave, this lot. You would have thought there was a hail of fire already spraying across the front yard. The ones behind the wall hit the ground so hard, I am sure some of them will take a while to get up.

Dad shuts the door and turns to the kid.

"You bastard!" he hisses. "I was trying to help you. Now see what you did!" The kid says nothing. Maybe he has realized his mistake. Maybe he hasn't. Maybe he is too scared to realize anything. He just sits there and shakes.

"He is gonna faint soon, I guess," Aisha says. "He looks kinda queasy."

"Must be hungry," says Mum from the kitchen doorway. She moves back into the kitchen. "I will cook something. I forgot to cook because of all this nonsense!"

True. If not for the delinquent, Mum would have been halfway to cooking something so nice that the kitchen would be filled with the aroma of the Orient and the table steadily filling with all kinds of dishes, fried, boiled, garnished. All delicious. Pity the delinquent had to spoil it all.

She walks into the kitchen and starts rummaging inside the fridge; I can hear pans clattering and then something being cut or sliced. I turn and there she is, busily cutting something, the veil still covering her face.

On the sofa the delinquent is also watching her. Suddenly he seems more preoccupied with her than with his own situation. Must be wondering what kind of a woman this is, all covered up, screaming at me when I have the gun and then screaming at her husband when he has it, and now cooking food as if nothing had happened. I can see that his fear and anger are giving way to curiosity.

"Does she ever take that thing off?" he asks suddenly, speaking to no one in particular. He means the *niqab*, of course.

I look at Aisha, who is rolling her eyes in disbelief. I am with her. What's with this guy? Doesn't he have other things to worry about right now?

But I answer. Mum always says it is our responsibility to educate unbelievers.

" 'Course she does," I say. "How do you think she is gonna take a shower?"

I can see the delinquent is not convinced. He probably thinks we are so strange we might have some weird way of taking showers without taking our clothes off.

"What's with the mouth thing?"

"It's called a *niqab*!" Now Aisha can't keep her mouth shut. "Not a mouth thing!" The delinquent looks at her as if he is cross with her for butting in. But it's Mum who tells her off.

"You mind your business, Aisha!" she cries from the kitchen. "Leave him alone!"

Aisha pouts. But the delinquent's curiosity is growing. He expresses it as a statement.

"Fucken weird," he mumbles, looking away.

Dad, who is at the window peering out, hears it and stares at him.

"What did you say?" he asks.

"He thinks we are fucking weird," Aisha tells

him. I guess she wants Dad to hit him again. I know I do. If anybody is "fucken weird," it's him. Coming into our house, shooting up everything, and now calling us weird. Fucken cheeky that is.

"Aisha!" cries Mum from the kitchen, and the kid looks at all of us like we are the delinquents.

"Fucken weird," he mumbles again, but more softly this time.

Dad is now truly spastic. He reaches the sofa in two steps, grabs the boy by his windcheater, and raises his fist like he is going to slam it into the idiot's face. I want him to. I really do. He can't come in here, threaten us, shoot up our house, and then abuse us, too. Especially now when we got the gun.

But Dad doesn't slam his fist down. He freezes, like he has had a change of heart. Then he places his face just inches from the thin, freckled face and hisses.

"You say that one more time, I will throw you in that fire, you bloody bastard!"

If the kid still thinks we are fucken weird, he doesn't say it any more. He stares at Dad's eyes and then looks away.

"Ignore him. Leave him alone!" Mum shouts

from the kitchen. "Think of a way to get rid of him without giving him to the police."

Dad looks in the direction of the kitchen and then at me and sighs. This is way too much for him. It's a bit much for me, too. Having to take all this abuse when we are the victims. God shouldn't have revealed so much to the Prophet. It only lets pious people get bullied.

Now Mum is also standing there beyond the doorway staring at the boy. She is not angry, though. She has the same look she has in her eyes when she finds that she has served me a full plate of rice and I have eaten only three-quarters of it.

The delinquent sees her and turns his eyes away. Just like I do when Mum looks at me like that.

SUDDENLY THERE IS A NOISE outside. Somebody is speaking again, through a megaphone. We listen carefully, and the voice is speaking in Dari.

"It's that bastard Mustafa!" Dad says, recognizing the voice. "What does he want?"

I look outside. Yes, it is Uncle Mustafa. He is standing near the wall with a megaphone in his hand, looking rather important. Don't tell me he has found a new and dramatic way to ask for the lawnmower!

But it seems that Uncle Mustafa doesn't want anything. The cops want him to speak to Dad, in Dari, and tell him exactly what the situation is like.

Dad puts his head out and speaks. "You don't need that thing to speak to me, you idiot!" he tells Uncle Mustafa in Dari. "How many times have you spoken to me from there without a megaphone?" Very true. Uncle Mustafa always speaks to us from near the wall, never with a megaphone.

But he only laughs. "These idiots want me to speak to you in our language," he says through the megaphone. "I saw the whole thing on TV and came up to see what is happening. Then they saw me and asked me to speak to you."

Obviously the coppers saw this Afghan-looking dude coming up the street and thought they could make use of him. The fact that Dad had only nodded earlier must have convinced them that they were dealing with an immigrant who spoke no English. But then, I guess, even if he had spoken, they would have still called for an interpreter. A lot of people are like that. If you have an accent, they think you can't speak.

"Tell the idiots I speak English."

Uncle Mustafa only shrugs his shoulders. "No point," he says. "They have made up their mind." That is scary. When cops make up their minds. That means everybody else can stop thinking. I am sure they have made up their minds about the delinquent, too. If only we could make up our minds about him.

But I am also frustrated by the mention of television. I can even see some of the TV people there now, behind the cop cars, filming. We must be all over it. Our street, our house, maybe even Dad is there right now as he speaks. Nadia must have seen it all! Oh my god! What must she be thinking! If only this idiot hadn't shot up the TV.

"Pity we can't watch TV," says Dad to Mustafa.

"Why?"

"The bastard shot up everything," Dad reveals. "The TV, the computer. He even took our phones and threw them in the fire."

Uncle Mustafa clicks his tongue. "Are you all right?" he asks. Maybe he thinks we are next to go into the fire. But I doubt if he is too concerned about that. As long as the mower is unhurt, he will be happy, I am sure.

The cops are getting a bit agitated now. The one who looks like the boss is looking impatiently at Mustafa and then back at Dad. They had asked the Afghan to speak to his countryman about the boy, and they seem to be having a nice little chitchat. I am relieved we are the only other Afghan family within megaphone range in the area. If not, at least Mustafa's part in the chat would not be so private.

A copper tells something to Uncle Mustafa, and he says something back apologetically. There is more cop-to-Mustafa communication before Mustafa speaks to us again.

"They want to know what is going on there."

Dad thinks for a few seconds. I hope he doesn't say what happened. Uncle Mustafa is notorious for spreading rumours. Before you know it, the *Herald Sun* will get hold of the story about us disarming the kid and keeping him away from the cops. Besides, Uncle Mustafa is one of them Afghans who thinks that although Allah may have given him his life, the Australian Government gives him his dole. So he might just tell the cops everything straight away, without bothering about the *Herald Sun*, just to show that he is on the side of those who give him free money rather than those who lend him their mower with free petrol. There are people like that. They will hand over their parents if they feel the dole is threatened.

"He is holding us hostage," Dad says finally,

deciding to risk God's wrath instead of Mustafa's trust. I guess he knows Mustafa well enough.

"Very tough guy. Don't think he will come out easily."

Uncle Mustafa translates to the copper. The cop tells him something.

"He wants you to keep him occupied," he says. "Until they come up with a plan."

Dad shakes his head. "Tell them not to try anything just yet," he says. "This guy might shoot us if they do."

Mustafa translates, and the cop listens. He nods vigorously to show both Mustafa and Dad that he understands.

"Are you in any danger now?"

"No," Dad says. "But if the coppers try something, we will be."

I can see Dad's getting the hang of this now. He knows exactly what to say. But it's also kind of sad in a way. He is telling one lie after another. How all this sits with God, I really don't know. You give refuge to the kid because that is what God wants, but then you lie to save him. Wouldn't God see that, too? But I don't want to think too much about that. That kind of thing only makes me go crazy. And also more angry at the delinquent for making Dad do this.

Maybe when all this is over, I will ask Mum. I can ask Dad, but he will only tell me to ask Mum anyway.

Near the fence, Mustafa continues to translate. The cop nods tiredly and takes the megaphone to show that he is not in need of Mustafa's interpretations any more.

Dad is about to take his head in when I remember something. "Ask him who won the footy."

I know Uncle Mustafa is no more reliable than Dad when it comes to footy, but he can ask the cops, I am sure. I don't know when this stupid drama will be over, and I am not going to wait so long to find out the footy scores.

Dad looks at me as if I were asking for extra pocket money after I have already been given ten bucks.

"Please?" That always works with pocket money. It works with the footy scores, too.

"Oi! Mustafa!" Dad calls out. "Ask them who won the footy."

Mustafa asks and tells us the answer.

"Carlton."

I pump my fist in the air. Dad looks at me triumphantly. Maybe now you will take me seriously, he seems to be saying.

But it's the delinquent who speaks.

"Carlton's shit!"

I look at him in disbelief. Does he ever give up trying to express himself? I look at Aisha, and the little shit is trying hard to suppress her laughter. She goes for Essendon. I want to tell them both where to go, but Dad gives me a look that says I should do what Mum says. Ignore him.

"How much longer to ignore this idiot?" I ask in Dari, and Mum calls out through the smell of the Orient: "As long as it takes for him to get tired. We are not going to keep him forever."

I certainly hope not. Imagine putting up with this cheek forever! The delinquent is looking at my father. I can see he is impatient.

"What do they want?"

"They want you to come out with your hands up in the air," Dad puts his arms in the air to show what he means. He even wriggles his fingers for added effect, a little wicked smile on his lips. The delinquent smirks contemptuously.

"They can fuck off!"

I can see that Dad is annoyed with the swearing, but he is less annoyed than before. I think instead of the delinquent getting tired, we are getting used to him and his tantrums. All because of the Koran.

Dad, however, has a trick up his sleeve. "They also want us to hand you over." He smiles again, evilly. I think he wants to see if he can intimidate him without hitting him. But the delinquent is not to be ruffled so easily any more. He smirks. I think he is beginning to get our measure just as we got his. We knew he was unlikely to shoot us when he shot the TV. I think he is getting the feeling that we are unlikely to hand him over.

"Rubbish!" he says. "They don't know you got the gun."

"You want us to tell them?" Aisha snaps from her corner. Good one! It clinches the argument as it makes the kid grind his lips and look away. But Mum bawls from the kitchen.

"Aisha!" she yells. "Mind your own business!" She is truly pissed off with us now.

I see a little grin passing over the delinquent's lips again.

He mumbles something, but too softly for us to

hear. Probably another "fucken weird" or something along those lines.

We settle back in our places, Dad near the widow keeping an eye on the cops and the delinquent and me on the sofa. I just stare at the idiot. He is now a bit relaxed, I guess, because he feels he is safe. He doesn't understand why, but he can sense he is safe, at least for the moment.

But I am worried. I just can't see where this is all heading. How long are we going to keep him here? What are we going to do with him? Mum says to ignore him until we find a way to get rid of him. But how can we get rid of him? There is, of course, a very easy way to do it—the coppers are just outside. But since we—or Mum—don't want to go against God, we have to find another way to deal with it. But how? I can't think of anything, and I can't see anybody else thinking of anything. Dad is busy watching the cops, and Mum is busy cooking. Aisha, well, she is busy watching the delinquent, even though all she can see is the back of his head.

And ignoring him isn't that easy, either. He is just sitting there right in our face, expressing himself whenever he feels like it.

"What are we gonna do with him?" I ask Dad again in Dari.

He shrugs and looks in the direction of the kitchen. I can see that he, too, is beginning to get worried.

"Think of something," Mum says from the kitchen. "Think of a plan before the police think of one."

That is easier said than done. And by the looks of it, Mum has given us the responsibility of thinking of a plan. She is too busy producing the aromas of the Orient.

Our talking has made the delinquent uneasy again. I guess he knows we are discussing him. He must be wondering whether we are going to give him up after all.

Suddenly he gets up. We all start. "I wanna take a leak."

We are relieved. He just wants to go to the toilet, not launch an unarmed assault on the cops outside. I point in the direction of the toilet, pleased that he is not going to leak all over the sofa and carpet, which, mind you, is quite possible. He just takes off. All that water must be ready to leave that skeletal body.

"Go with him," Dad says. "Don't leave him alone." I look at him in disbelief. Surely he doesn't want me to really be with him?

"Make sure he goes in the toilet," Dad provides additional information.

He must be worried that the nutter might sneak out of the house.

I go to the toilet. The door is closed. I stand outside the door listening. Nothing.

"Oi!" I call. "Are you in there?"

There is no answer, but after a few seconds I can hear the piss falling like a torrent.

He walks out a few seconds later.

"Don't call me 'oi,' " he says, zipping up and looking at me like I have sworn at him or something. "I have a name."

Dad looks at me and then at the delinquent. There is a little grin on Dad's lips. I can see he is becoming quite amused by the kid's spirit. I guess you got to hand it to him. We have the gun, we are in control, the cops are just a shout away, and he still snaps at us.

"Well, what *is* your name?" Dad asks.

I suddenly realize, like Dad did I am sure, that we don't know his name. I am sure the TV mentioned it in the morning, but then who remembers that?

Dad waits for an answer. The kid looks at him as if wondering whether to answer the question or just be rude as usual. He decides quickly.

"Russell," he says grumpily. "But everyone calls me Rusty." We all look at each other as if we can't believe our ears.

Rusty? Then we all laugh, even Mum from the kitchen. How can we not? Not only do we have an Afghan Rusty, we now have an Aussie one, too.

The kid stares at us, utterly confused. Dad explains. "I am also called Rusty," he says, quite proudly. "My real name is Rustum Ahmed Khan, but Australians call me Rusty." He grins happily. Then he does something truly weird, even for him. He goes on to introduce all of us. "My son is Khalid, my daughter Aisha, and of course my wife Mehri, which means 'kind and affectionate.' "

But it only confuses the boy. Suddenly we are treating him like a guest, introducing ourselves. He probably still thinks we are fucking weird. Must be even wondering if he has stepped into a different house through the toilet.

But for us, suddenly, he is not just irritating any

more. He is interesting, too. "Rusty!" Mum says to herself from the kitchen doorway, looking at the kid, shaking her head in disbelief, and smiling. Near the table, Aisha giggles.

Rusty is now clearly irritated by the attention. He is not sure whether we are genuinely amused or we are taking the piss out of him. He sits back down on the sofa and sulks.

Dad sits on the sofa in front of Rusty and looks at him, the smile still on his lips. He is looking at him as if he has just discovered him. I guess we all feel a bit like that now. In a way, we have discovered him. As Rusty.

But Rusty is not amused by the attention. He looks at Dad as if Dad is pushing his luck.

Dad is. "Well, Rusty," he asks, "what did you do to go to prison?"

I wonder if this is really necessary to ask. Okay, he is an interesting character, with a cool nickname, but does that mean we got to know his life story? He is still the guy who threatened us and shot up our TV. I think we still ought to keep a bit of distance. Dad seems to think otherwise. He is sitting there, drawn to his namesake, waiting for a reply to his question. He looks like a kid who has suddenly discovered that a textbook he thought to be boring actually contains some cool pictures. Maybe he is also thinking that if the boy's going to be here for a while, we might as well get to know him, especially now that we also know he has a cool name. But he is keen. I can tell that.

Rusty senses that, too, and I can also tell he is not very happy with that. He looks at Dad with the same grumpy look he had given me when he came out of the toilet. I get the feeling that he is going to say something really rude, something like "none of your fucking business," when he surprises us.

"For assault," he says, tone flat.

"Oh!" Dad clicks his tongue.

I stare at Rusty. Assault? Him? He doesn't look like someone who can defend himself, let alone assault somebody. But then, who knows! He doesn't look like somebody who would walk into a house and try to take a family hostage with a gun, but he did. Except he picked the wrong family.

"Who did you assault?"

Rusty is getting impatient with the interrogation, but he answers. "A copper."

I look at Aisha and see her looking at me with wide eyes. A copper! Wow! Is he for real?

"No kidding!" I say to him. "A copper?"

Wow! This was totally unexpected. You always want to assault a cop, but you never have the courage. Now you meet somebody who says he's done what you have wanted to do but didn't have the guts for. And now I am totally with Dad. I got to know more about this dude.

"Yeah," answers Rusty. He is suddenly sensing that he has an audience for a reason other than him just being here. It kind of relaxes him. I can see that in the way he leans back in the sofa.

"Why?" I guess if you are a teenager, you don't really have to ask why anybody would bash a copper, but I ask anyway.

"He was an asshole to me and a mate."

"And they sent you to jail for that?" Dad asks. Maybe he thinks he should have been given a medal or something. I cannot agree more. Cops are always asking to be assaulted, if you ask me. If I had assaulted a copper each time one had asked us to move off when we make a bit of noise in the mall or the street, I would be doing life several times over now I reckon. I don't think Dad has had any experience like that, but you don't have to tell an Afghan about coppers here. The way they look at you, especially when you are wearing the Islamic dress, tells you a lot about what they think. A medal? I say give him a job as a consultant to all teenagers—and Afghans—wanting to teach a copper a lesson.

Rusty wants to clarify things, though. "Nah, it's not just that," he says. "I had a few previous as well."

I see. A boy with a criminal record. Did I say he was not just a freckled face?

"Why did you shoot the guard in the prison?"

"Cuz he tried to stop me." He looks at Dad as if he had asked a stupid question. "And he was a prick anyway."

We sit there looking at the boy. Suddenly he looks like more than a rude, offensive boy. He has a name, a funny one at that, and he has solid achievements to his name.

"Where'd you get the gun from?"

"A mate gave it to me." Another "Are you really stupid or what?" look follows.

We watch him silently for a few minutes. He certainly is a piece of work, our Rusty. Seems to think that assaulting a copper, going to jail, getting a gun, shooting a prison officer, busting out of jail, invading a house are all in a day's work. Our fascination with the person beneath that skinny, freckled frame is growing. I wonder what else he is going to reveal about himself.

We don't have to wait long.

"What about your family?" Dad asks, very seriously. The inevitable question, I guess. You meet someone who has had a violent past, you want to know what kind of family he has, even if you feel a bit excited about the mischief he has caused. But I guess the answer is also predictable.

"I have no family," Rusty says. I can see he is trying to sound as if he didn't care, but he can't hide the fact that he does. The voice goes slightly soft at the edge.

Dad looks puzzled. But only for a moment. Then he realizes what Rusty means and nods. He stares at the floor as if thinking of something to say. I can imagine what he is thinking. Abusive parents, broken family, poor education, no God in life. The kid must have gone through hell. I can appreciate all those things, too, except the God bit. I have seen lots of people having a good life without God. Not that it ever makes me lose faith in God, but I believe you can have a good life without Him, at least in this life. But you can't without good parents.

Then, after a few seconds where the stupid clock takes over again, Rusty speaks.

"My mum was a bitch," he says softly and quickly looks in the direction of the kitchen to see if Mum overheard. He sees Mum looking and suddenly seems embarrassed. The freckles glow.

"Does she understand English?"

I can't help smiling. We have heard this question from lots of people. So I give the same answer we have given them.

"Yeah, it's probably better than yours."

If Rusty is annoyed, he doesn't show it. He just grinds his lips together and looks away. A male pout.

Dad turns the conversation back to the original topic. "So she was bad, huh?" He is intrigued by Rusty's condemnation of his mum. I am, too. But to me the bigger puzzle is what his dad would have been like. If his mum was a bitch, we can only imagine what the dad would have been like. Probably a wolf.

Rusty nods at Dad's question. He doesn't seem to mind answering. Maybe he likes the attention.

Maybe he likes to talk about his family to somebody other than some official.

"She was," he says. "The biggest bitch in town."

"And your dad?" I ask, bracing for the answer.

"He was a good bloke," Rusty says, disappointing me. "The best. He loved us. He was just too fucken weak against her."

I stare at him. This is most intriguing. I look at Dad and then at Aisha and Mum, who is still at the kitchen door. They all look stumped. Why shouldn't they be?

This is the first time we have heard something like this, mum being a bitch and the dad too weak against her.

Rusty senses our confusion and decides to clear things. "My mum drank a lot," he explains. "A fucken lot. And she slept around with a lot of men. Didn't care about me or my brother or my dad." He pauses as if it's already too much for him. "My dad was a good bloke. But he was very timid. And small. My mother was a big woman. She treated my dad like shit. She would get into fits and hit my father, sometimes with anything she could find."

His voice is rising with the emotions. The

swearing is a bit too strong, but we are too inter-ested in the content of the story to mind the style of presentation.

"And your dad could do nothing?"

"No," Rusty says firmly. "I said he was small and weak, and he was a very gentle bloke, too."

"And you couldn't do anything, either?"

Rusty swallows hard. "No!" he snaps. He seems annoyed that we are asking all these questions when the answers are so obvious to him. "I told you, she was fucken scary. She beat us, too. My little brother ran away from her, and we never found him."

I take a deep breath. What kind of world is this, I wonder. A mother beating the father and the son running away from her. I just cannot imag-ine what a monster that woman must have been. Thank God I have my Mum, who is big and strong but loves us big and strong, too.

It's my Dad who puts it into words, though.

"*Hamdulillah*, my wife is big and strong, too, but she never drinks, and she has no lovers be-sides me."

And he chuckles softly. I guess he couldn't resist that. I can't help smiling, either, and I see there is even a slight smile on Rusty's lips as he glances in the direction of the kitchen. Mum has gone back in, but her reply comes out in no time.

"Stop treating this like a joke. If you think you are so lucky, show more respect!" She is trying to sound angry, but I can sense she is not. She likes it when my father jokes about her, in a way that compliments her, of course. They have been together long enough to know their respect for each other, I guess.

Done with his little joke, Dad returns to Rusty. "Is your dad still with your mum?"

"No, after I got jailed, I heard she kicked him out." What a woman!

"And where is he now?"

Rusty looks at Dad, then at me, and then glances at the kitchen again.

"Last I heard was that he moved to this side of the city." He pauses and looks around, the way one does before delivering some really startling news.

"To this street."

We all look at each other. This street? Rusty's meek and mild dad here? On this street?

"This street?"

Rusty sticks his hand into his pocket and pulls out something. It's an envelope, old and crumpled. He shows it to us.

"That's the address."

We look at it. Yes, it is this street. But the address . . . it's the house at the end, near the little park. The one opposite Mustafa's.

I look at Dad.

"That is where your father lives?"

"Yes."

We look at each other again, as the meaning of what he says sinks in. So Little Barry, the little bloke who lived in that house, was Rusty's abused father? The bloke who harmed nobody but himself with his drink. No wonder he drank himself to death. Losing his self-respect and his children to a mad cow with the drinking disease.

And then, suddenly, other things also begin to make sense. Rusty is not just running away from prison, I realize. He is running away to his father, probably the only person who matters to him in the world.

And he is dead.

Obviously, Rusty doesn't know it.

"Do you know him?" he asks, seeing the confusion—and the recognition—in our faces. "Do you know where he is?"

I am wondering what to say when Dad answers.

"Your dad is not there any more, Rusty," he says gravely, leaning forward and touching Rusty's arm. "He is now with God."

To all those adults who wish to console kids—or even adults—who have lost loved ones with the lame "He's with God now," please don't. The last thing someone wants to know is that the person they have lost is somewhere else, whether with God or not, when all they want is for that person to be with them. It doesn't matter if you think being with God is the ultimate. Heaven is far from home.

And Rusty is predictably shaken. "What are you saying?" he asks. I guess he is confused, too. But not enough to miss the fundamental truth behind his dad going to God.

"You mean he is . . . "

"Dead." I tell him. Bluntly. I think the boy ought to know the truth plainly. I would like that if my Dad passed away. I wouldn't want some stranger to tell me with a very grave face, "Khalid, nothing to worry boy, because your old man is up there in heaven." It sounds so dishonest.

Rusty now stares at us. He doesn't believe it. Dad stares at me as if he can't believe it, either. That I could have been so blunt.

"I don't believe it," Rusty says, but his voice is breaking, and I know he is fighting not to believe.

"Well," I tell him, " 'tis true. He passed away a coupla weeks ago." Dad nods. He is happier with my follow-up technique.

"How?"

"Heart failure," Dad says, pointing to his chest. He glances at me, daring me to contradict him. We all know Little Barry drank himself to death. But then it is also possible he drank himself to death after his heart broke.

"No one informed me."

I guess no one knew who he was or who his son was. It happens sometimes, especially here where family members don't want to know each other sometimes. Hell, we didn't know he was dead until Mustafa discovered him on one of his lawn-mowing jobs. He must have been dead for a few days by then. It was the smell that attracted Mustafa to the body.

But I don't want to tell Rusty that. There is a limit to being blunt.

Rusty looks at the floor, clutching the envelope. I can see his shoulders heaving with his chest; I can't see his eyes, but I know there are tears in them. "It's God's will," says Dad. "There is nothing we can do. It's God's will."

"Fuck God!" Rusty says through the tears, which have now begun to flow freely.

Normally, Dad would have given him a thundering smack for saying that. Normally, I would punch his lights out for saying that. Normally, Aisha would have been all over him, scratching and clawing and doing whatever girls do when they get mad, forgetting all about keeping her distance from strange males. Normally, only Mum, with her respect for God and contempt for all those who doubt Him, would have ignored him. But this is not normal, we all know. There are enough tears in those words to tell us that there is pain behind the anger, pain we can only guess. Hell, you bust out of prison to see the only person who matters to you to find that he is dead, and somebody tells you it's God's will. How would you feel about God then?

But, then, God works in mysterious ways. Just when you are about to abandon hope in Him, He shows that He is present, often in the most casual way.

My Mum who has been listening to everything from the kitchen now appears with a big plate of rice and meat and places it on the coffee table with a fork and spoon. Her *niqab* is off.

"Eat!" she says. In English.

We all look up. Rusty looks up with eyes still pumping tears, his freckled cheeks washed by them. He can't believe what he has heard, and he can't believe what he sees. He wants to say something, but he can't.

"Eat!" Mum says again in English. She waits till Rusty picks up the fork and walks back to the kitchen.

"Your food is here, if you want," she calls us over her shoulder.

Lunch is a silent affair. I guess nobody is in the mood to say anything, especially Rusty. All he does is sniffle, which he does every few seconds. The tissues are disappearing fast. So is the food. The grief is not preventing Rusty from eating like he has not eaten for a week.

Maybe he hasn't, at least for a day since he busted out of prison. And it's hard to resist Mum's cooking anyway.

We sit around and eat in silence, me and Dad sitting in the lounge with Rusty. Aisha eats at the dining table. Mum waits for us to finish so that she can eat. She always does. Nobody has ever told her to, but that is what she does. It is hard to change people like that.

Outside, the cops are quiet. We have been so absorbed in Rusty's life story that we have forgotten completely about the cops. But there is nothing to worry about. They are all over the place, yes, but they are quiet. Must be still thinking of a plan.

But the silence lasts only a few minutes. Suddenly, the chopper appears. Again. I really don't know what those idiots want. Are they trying to scare Rusty into giving himself up by threatening to land on top of him? That's what it sounds like. The stupid thing coming to land on top of the roof.

Rusty is upset. Worried. The sound of the chopper makes him nervous. Hell, it makes all of us nervous, but Rusty's hands are shaking. He can't get the fork to pick up the meat, and his face has gone all tight.

Suddenly, he looks up and yells.

"Go away!" he screams. "Go away, you bastards! Leave me alone!"

That is pointless. The chopper can't hear him. But it doesn't stop him. He gets up and starts pacing the lounge, looking up, putting his hands to his ears like he wants to stop the noise, but it's pointless.

I hear Mum calling from the kitchen. "Is Mustafa still there?" she asks.

Dad peers out and nods.

I hear the kitchen window opening and then Mum calling out. In Dari. "Mustafa!" she yells. "Tell these idiots to take this machine away. It's making him nervous, and he will shoot us all!"

We can't hear what Uncle Mustafa says, but in a few moments we hear the chopper moving off.

The power of Mum.

5 RUSTY RETURNS TO HIS PLATE of rice and meat. He continues his meal while drinking more water. Now there is a permanent glass of water near him.

I watch him. He is still sniffling but not as much as he did a while ago. Settling down, I guess. I decide to help him.

"Do you like that?" I ask, pointing to the food. I guess this is not a good time to ask whether he likes anything that he is eating. He is so hungry he will like anything. Even the plate. But I still feel like making conversation. It will do him good, I think.

"Yeah," he mumbles through a mouthful.

"Fucken awesome." He swallows and takes another sip of water. "And smells nice, too."

"The aroma of the Orient," I tell him. I had to say it. So tempting. He doesn't stop eating but glances at me like he is sizing me up.

"What?"

"Forget it," I say. It was a stupid thing to say to Rusty but in a way worth it just to see that expression on his face.

At the table, Aisha is shaking her head, suppressing a laugh. Rusty quickly glances in her direction and then at me.

"You takin' the piss outta me or something?"

Even in the midst of his sorrow, Rusty has fight in him. "Leave him alone!" Mum cries from the kitchen.

I leave him alone but only for a minute. His spirit is like one of them rubber balls that pop up no matter how deep you sink it. I can't help but like it.

"What is prison like?"

"Shit," he says. As simple as that.

"You got TV there?"

"Yeah," he says. "Cable."

I look at the blasted TV. "We have cable but no TV," I say with a grin.

Rusty glances at the TV. He grins sheepishly.

"Sorry," he mumbles. "My bad."

You can't help but be fascinated by him. An hour ago, I would have throttled him, but now it would seem like the destruction of an endangered species.

"How much was it?"

"Two thousand Australian dollars," Dad declares from the window. My Dad pronounces Australia "Awusthraalia." He does it very proudly. Probably thinks it's the correct way to pronounce it, too.

"Sorry" is all that Rusty says. I guess that's all that he can do. Not like he is going to pay it back or anything. It's a huge loss for us, I admit, especially the TV and the phones, but then it's nothing compared to what he has lost.

He finishes the food, scraping off the last bit with the fork. I look in the direction of the kitchen.

"Mum!" I cry. "We need another serve here!"

Out comes Mum with another heaped plate of meat and rice. Rusty's face lights up.

"Ta," he says with a shy grin. The boy is not just a freckled face and a bottomless stomach. He has manners, too.

Then he attacks the food. Aisha giggles softly in the background, and Mum frowns at her as she walks back to the kitchen.

"So what do you do in prison?" I continue from where I left.

"Bugger all," Rusty picks up from where he left.

"You have a gym?"

"Yeah."

Obviously he doesn't use it. Those skinny arms look strong, but they are not the strength from lifting weights.

"Which school did you go to?"

He tells the name of a secondary school that could be any of hundreds of dumps that pass as schools. Ours is not that better, but at least it's a private dump.

"What was it like?"

"A dump," Rusty says, confirming my judgement. And there is that look again. Are you stupid or something?

"Which footy team you go for?"

"Essendon."

I quickly look at Aisha, who is sticking her tongue out at me. She does that so often. I remember when we were younger, I used to tell her to put it away or I would cut it off with the scissors. That's how annoying it is.

"Oh, really?" I say. "So does my sister."

Rusty looks at her over his shoulder. He seems interested in her for the first time. The power of footy.

"That's cool," he says. "Who is ya fave player?" he asks her.

Aisha glances in the direction of the kitchen to see if Mum is watching. Dad is watching her, but she knows the power of Mum is greater than the power of Dad and footy put together. Confident that Mum is not looking, she answers.

"Howlett."

"Yeah, he is good," Rusty agrees and returns to his food.

"Aisha!" cries Mum from the kitchen.

"Howlett is shit." I have to say that. For the sake of my team, even though I think Howlett is good.

"Howlett is better than all of Carlton shits put together," Rusty sneers through a mouthful of rice. I look at Aisha, and she is rapt. If she keeps sticking her tongue out like that I might be tempted to bring the scissors and cut it off after all.

Rusty looks at her again and then at me. "Why doesn't she wear the mouth thing?"

"*Niqab!*" corrects Aisha.

"Aisha!" yells Mum. She is obviously not happy about Aisha getting too cosy with Rusty and Howlett. Mum wouldn't know Howlett from Harry, but she knows we are talking about footy players and that footy players are young men running around in skimpy shorts. Not the kind of thing a Muslim girl should get excited about, at least not in her presence.

Aisha pouts, but before that she pokes her tongue out at me again to rub in her advantage at finding another Essendon fan.

Dad sees no need to worry about Howlett, as the conversation has been now diverted to the *niqab*.

"It's her choice," he explains. "Allah doesn't force people to do things."

"Who is Allah?" Rusty wants to know.

"Allah is God."

He looks at me, then Dad, and then at me again. He is confused enough to stop eating.

"Then why don't you just call him God?"

What a kid!

" 'Allah' is Arabic for God. That is where Islam was born. In Arabia," I teach him. These infidels need to be handled gently.

But Rusty looks at me as if trying to figure out if this is another "aroma of the Orient" kind of statement. Then he shrugs his shoulders and goes back to eating.

He finishes his meal and takes another drink. Then he gets up and takes the plate towards the kitchen.

"Where are you going?"

"To wash the plate," he says, looking at me as if I had asked a stupid question.

Mum comes out and takes the plate. "Give it to me," she says in Dari. "I wash plates here."

"I can wash it," he says stubbornly in English. We are sure he can wash a plate. A boy who shoots a prison guard, busts out of prison, comes all the way to where his dad lives, and then shoots up a neighbour's house must be able to wash a plate. But that is not the way we do things here.

"Mum says she washes the plates here."

Rusty looks at Mum, and Mum points to the sofa.

"Go sit," she says again, in English. Rusty returns to his seat. I swear he looks like a little kid, doing what his mum says. I bet his mum never did that for him, washing his plates. I don't think she even cooked for him by the sound of it.

"He is sweet," Mum says, switching back to the language of her ancestors.

"Yes," agrees Dad, taking a peek outside. "Not like bloody Mustafa. He is being a bloody bastard outside."

I look out. Dad's right. There is Mustafa talking to some TV people. There must be at least a dozen of them with cameras and microphones surrounding Mustafa, who is speaking non-stop. I can see the police are getting irritated with him. The boss cop is looking at him while talking to his troops, and his look says that he has made a huge mistake by getting the wandering Afghan to translate. But Mustafa is enjoying it. You can see from the way he is throwing his arms about. The TV people don't seem to have any complaints, either. Where else can you find such an obliging commentator?

If only we had the TV, we could have watched it all. Live. Rusty is back on the sofa now. He is taking little sips from his water glass, thinking.

God knows he has a lot to think about. At least he is not crying any more. My little exchange with him about bugger all has distracted him from real issues. At least that's what I'd like to think.

But he is back to base quickly.

"Did you know my dad well?" he asks Dad.

"No, not that well," Dad answers. "Mustafa knew him very well, though. They were neighbours." He points his thumb in the direction of the road where Mustafa is standing, delivering a running commentary to the press. I wonder what Mustafa would think if he knew that Rusty is Little Barry's son. Might want to come in and tell him all about his father and what a good neighbour he was to Barry.

"He was a good bloke," I say to Rusty. But I guess he already knew that.

I see the tears welling in his eyes again. He wipes his nose on his sleeve. One tissue box is already down, with a pile of wet, snotty tissues heaped on the floor. Dad goes to the kitchen table and gets another box, telling me in Dari to clean up the mess on the floor. I gather the tissues and yesterday's junk mail under the coffee table and take them all to the kitchen and dump them in the bin. The tissues are heavy. There is a lot of sorrow sticking to them.

But there is more to come. As Dad gives the second box to Rusty, he pulls out a handful of tissues and blows his nose so hard that I am sure it would have disturbed Mustafa's sermon on the road.

"What are you going to do with me?" Rusty asks, glancing at Dad.

Good question. We had not thought about it for a while, busy as we were with Rusty's life story. I think now it's time we had a serious thought about it.

I look straight at Dad, who looks straight at Mum, who is now at the kitchen table eating. "Don't look at me!" she says. "Think of something."

"We will think of something," Dad conveys the gist of our quick family discussion to Rusty.

He looks worried. Dad's the same. I guess he realizes we can't postpone making a decision forever. Mum is too busy eating, before she gets busy washing the dishes, to think about it. Aisha is still basking in the knowledge of Rusty being an Essendon supporter.

"So you are not going to give me to the cops?" Rusty asks, looking from me to Dad and then at Mum in the kitchen.

I am sure he must have realized by now that we are not likely to give him over to the cops, even if he doesn't know what we are going to do with him. But I guess he needs to make sure.

"No," says Dad. "We are not."

"It's against our religion," I tell him gravely.

Rusty looks confused again. What kind of religion is this, he must be wondering. I walk into their home and threaten them and shoot their TV and computer, and they don't want to give me to the cops because it is against their religion? He must think we are truly fucken weird. I would have thought so, too, if I were not Muslim.

"We are Muslims," Dad declares proudly. "And Afghans. It is against our religion and culture to give up somebody who is at our mercy."

"And you are at our mercy," I remind him.

Rusty is still not sure what is going on. He looks at Mum in the kitchen, and Mum nods very hard, which probably means that, yes, I agree it is against our religion and, yes, I agree you are at our mercy.

"It is against God's wishes to turn in a fugitive."

Rusty nods. I still don't think he gets it, but I am sure he likes what he hears.

"I guess you thought we are all terrorists, huh?"

I can't help asking. I have to. Too many people think Muslims are nothing but a bunch of lunatics going around blowing up people.

Probably Rusty did, too, but he doesn't say so. He has questions, though.

"Who does the bombs then?"

So he knows a bit about current events. I guess if you watch TV, you will, and in prison what else can you do? TV only shows Muslims who are terrorists or terrorist suspects. And if they have cable TV, man, that's like triple the dose!

Dad remains calm in the face of Rusty's educated question. "Terrorists!" he answers without any hesitation.

Rusty looks truly confused. He must be wondering who are the Muslims and who are the terrorists. I don't blame him. I get confused myself sometimes, especially when I listen to some of my friends. They want to do horrible things to certain people, the Jews, for instance. I am not a big fan of Jews myself, but I guess after what Hitler did to them, there is nothing much we can do. And aren't we supposed to be peace-loving and all that?

Dad decides to help him, in his own style.

"Some terrorists are also Muslims," he explains. "But we are better."

I can hear Aisha giggling even before Dad finishes, and I can't help smiling myself. Dad is totally capable of doing this. You ask him a question, and his answer leaves you even more confused than before. From the kitchen, Mum thunders.

"Don't confuse him," she says. "Tell him some Muslims think it's all right to kill, but it is wrong." She pokes her head out of the door and waits for me to translate.

I do.

Rusty just looks at us blankly. "So," he asks, "Muslims are not terrorists?"

Mum has to call Aisha to the kitchen to control her laughter. I look at Dad, who looks at me totally helpless. It is clear he agrees with me that religion and terrorism are too complicated for Rusty, never mind his own contribution to confusing him.

"Do you want some fruits?" Dad asks, bringing the discussion to Rusty's level. Rusty has already had two big plates of rice and meat, but he nods.

Mum, who has been watching from the kitchen, promptly brings the bowl of fruit from the kitchen table.

"Ta," he says, picking up a big banana. I hold out my hand for the peel, and while I take it to the kitchen, the banana disappears into Rusty's mouth.

6 It's just past twelve. We are still in the lounge, waiting. Nothing much has happened in the last couple of hours. Rusty is still here, and the cops are still outside. The only thing that has changed is that Rusty is sleeping. On the couch. I guess he was dead tired. He must have been if he had been on the run for such a long time. And if he wasn't, the stress of breaking into our house and trying to take us hostage and the shock of the news about his dad must have been enough to exhaust him.

"He looks so young," Mum says, looking at him as she passes him to the toilet.

"He is young," I point out. Well, he is. I don't

think he even has a proper beard growing on his cheeks yet.

"I mean, he is too young for the things that have happened to him."

I have to agree. At seventeen, he has been to prison, is without a family, and now is holed up here surrounded by cops and a crazy chopper pilot. It couldn't get any worse at his age, I guess. Well, not really. I have seen kids in Afghanistan who are worse off. No parents, no family, and not even their own two arms, living on charity. And much younger than Rusty. Living without almost everything they were born with, except their lives. But for Rusty this must be terrible, too. What has he got to look forward to?

Mum goes into our bedroom and brings my coverlet. She puts it over the sleeping Rusty and tucks the edge under his chin. It's not that cold. In fact, the fire is roaring, having long consumed our mobiles. But Mum seems to think Rusty needs to keep warm. She used to do that to me when I was younger, come into the room at night and tuck the end of the blanket under my chin. Now she just tells me to cover myself warmly, but I am sure she checks during the night.

"What a funny name," she says to Dad. "Rusty!" She giggles, and so does Aisha. My Mum can giggle very well. Sometimes Dad makes some joke about her, and she gives him a very stern look. But before that she giggles.

Rusty feels Mum's hand under his chin and starts. He grabs her arm like someone's about to throttle him or something but sees it's just Mum. He quickly lets her hand go and looks around. He looks like a drunken man, groggy and tired, looking through eyes heavy with sleep, the dirty blond hair all messy on his head. It's so funny that it makes us all laugh. Rusty doesn't see the joke. He looks confused for a moment and then looks at Mum again. Mum puts her folded hands to the side of her face and indicates he should go back to sleep. Rusty is too tired to say or do anything except manage a little grin before he closes his eyes.

"He must be dead tired."

Mum goes back to where she came from. The kitchen. Then, I see the envelope. It's on the floor near the sofa. I look at Dad, and he motions me to pick it up. We know it is not nice to read somebody else's mail, but we are curious. Surely God will forgive us these little things. We have saved the boy from the cops. I am sure we are entitled to a bit of his privacy.

"Dear Rusty," Little Barry starts, "thancs for your last letter. I am sory I couldn't come to see ya last weak. Something came up, but I will see ya next weak without fail. I have moved to this house now. Nice area. Gud naybors. You will like it when ya get out. Look after yaself. Keep out of trouble. I will see ya next weak."

I can tell Barry wasn't much of a writer. The spelling is pretty creative. Thancs! That is exactly how Aisha used to write it, until I corrected the silly girl after laughing at the mistake countless times. Even then the little brat wasn't convinced until I showed her the correct spelling in a book, even though I have always done better than her in English at school! I bet Little Barry didn't have an older brother like me. If he did, he would have been spelling right and writing longer letters, at least at his age. Uncle Mustafa would have been over the moon with the letter, though. That "gud naybor" bit was certainly about him. Obviously, Barry didn't know he was being a good neighbour with our petrol.

And no wonder Barry did not go to see Rusty. The letter was dated three weeks ago, a week before they found his body. I guess Rusty must have been pretty cut up when his old man didn't turn up for several weeks. I can only imagine how bad it must have been. Bad enough to want to get out and see him, I guess.

I see Aisha inching her way from the table towards us. I guess she wants to have a look at the letter, too. And maybe even get a closer look at Rusty. But Dad shoos her away, and she returns to the table with a mighty pout.

I feel sorry for her. Poor thing, she is like in a prison there behind the table. Can't move, can't say much. I guess it's not all that cool to be a daughter after all. I take the letter to her and show it to her. She reads it and looks at me and then at the sleeping Rusty. I know she is sad, because I can see the eyelids fluttering. She can get very sentimental. Usually, I tease her for that, but not today. Not now.

Mum comes out of the kitchen, almost on tiptoe for fear of waking Rusty. She takes the letter and reads it. Barry's English is simple enough for her. She shakes her head sadly and goes and looks at Rusty before going back to the kitchen. I guess she will start cooking something else for him now.

"Somebody's coming," Dad says suddenly.

We can hear footsteps outside. I look out, and there is a young woman approaching. Mid-twenties, fairly tall, brown hair, wearing jeans and jumper. Not really hot but good looking in a mature sort of way.

"Who is it? What does she want? " I ask Dad.

She wants to talk to us it seems, to talk to Rusty. She even calls him Rusty.

So this was the coppers' plan. To send a young woman to talk to the young boy and see if she could get him to come out, hands in the air, gun on the ground.

Rusty is also up now. The talking and the woman calling him have woken him. He is looking around, bleary-eyed, like he had just got out of a coma or something. It seems he is a bit confused, maybe he had been dreaming that he was still in prison. But then he sees us and remembers.

The woman calls again. She is looking very casual, but you can tell that she is a copper miles away. Must be one of them negotiators. Trained to handle situations like this. The casual dress must be part of the training.

She calls again and wants to speak to Rusty. But Rusty knows all about cops, I guess.

"Fuck off!" is all he says at the top of his voice from the sofa. "Fuck off or I'll shoot the lot of them."

The woman starts at the sudden shouting. But she is stubborn. She is not fucking off so easily as Rusty expects.

"I understand what you are going through, Rusty," she says. "But this is not the way to deal with it."

She is calm, but she talks as if she has rehearsed the whole thing. I guess she has. She is trained to do this. But it also makes her appear fake. The concern is fake, the tone is fake, the facial expressions are all fake. I guess even the clothes she is wearing are fake. Just another copper doing the job she is trained to do.

"Fuck off!" Rusty cries again. He is not trained to say that. He just says what's in his mind. Like any kid.

Dad puts his head out the window slightly.

"Please go away," he pleads. "You can't do anything. He is under a lot of stress. What he is saying now is all that you are going to hear."

"That's okay. I understand," she persists. "I am willing to talk him through this." I guess she wants to show that she is tough. And she looks at Dad like she is looking at a kid who doesn't know what he is talking about. I guess she thinks what does this stupid Afghan know about negotiations, but she is too well trained to say it. She just shows it.

Dad just looks at her, helpless. "If you keep trying to talk to him, he will shoot us all."

The woman looks at Dad. She seems unsure. Maybe she is wondering whether it is such a bad thing after all. A few Muslims dead and the boy captured at the end of it. But I am sure she knows it's bad for her, too. All that training and you end up with a dead family, even if it's a family of Muslims.

"It doesn't have to be like this," the woman continues the one-sided negotiation. "We can talk things over. Things are never as bad as they seem."

Dad is truly helpless now. "He is under a lot of stress. He has had a very hard time," he whines. "Please go away. You are going to get us all into a lot of trouble."

The woman is now looking at Dad as if she suspects something. It would be a surprise if she didn't. I mean, Dad is beginning to sound more and more like a spokesperson for Rusty rather than a hostage.

I look at Rusty. He is standing there behind Dad, fuming. "Why the fuck doesn't she go away?"

"You tell her again," I egg him on. I can't let Dad give the game away. He is very close. I can feel it and see it in the woman's eyes.

Rusty doesn't need much telling. He yells at the top of his voice.

"Go away, you silly bitch, or I will blow your brains off!"

That was the wrong thing to say. Threatening to blow a copper's brains off on top of having shot a prison guard, not to mention the assault on a copper that landed him in prison in the first place. But it has the effect that we were looking for. The well-trained negotiator is taken aback. She looks truly pissed off for a moment but recovers quickly to show a brave front. But her feet are telling something else. They move her in the direction of her colleagues, slowly but surely.

And in the street I can see Mustafa looking at

Dad and pointing to his head with his finger and circling it in an unmistakable gesture. The woman has lost it, he seems to be saying. I can see the boss cop glaring at him. If Mustafa is not careful, they will arrest him soon.

But Dad is relieved to see the woman retreat. He was so close to giving the game away. He lets out a huge sigh and is about to pull his head in when he remembers something.

"Oi, Mustafa!" he calls in Dari. "You know if that bastard Massoud knows about this?"

I am sure Dad knows that Massoud knows about it by now. The whole state must know. But I guess he just wants to make sure. What's going on at the shop must have been in the back of his mind all this time.

Mustafa gestures as if telling Dad not to worry.

"He knows," he assures. "He came here earlier, but the cops are not allowing anybody close to the house. So he went home to watch it on TV." He looks around proudly. "I am the only outsider they are allowing here."

That is not strictly true. I am sure the cops just don't know how to get rid of him.

But Dad is now worried about the shop.

"Bloody bastard!" he says, meaning of course Massoud. "Going home to watch television!"

He sits down heavily. He is not a happy man. I think the whole thing is beginning to get to him. The shop is just adding one more pile of shit to the heap that is already there. I wonder if he is really going to fire Massoud this time.

Again we settle down to wait. Rusty is not going back to sleep. He sits there, a worried look on his face. The negotiator has upset him, reminding him that the police are still there, trying to get him out.

"What are you going to do?" he asks again.

Dad looks at Mum. Eye communication.

"We don't know," Dad translates. "We don't want to give you up. It is not right."

Rusty seems relieved, but only slightly. I guess he needs to know a bit more about his fate, like what we are really going to do with him if we are not handing him over to the cops. But we don't have any ideas.

It's one o'clock, and Dad is praying. I wait for him to pray so that I can pray while he watches the cops. Mum and Aisha have already prayed in the kitchen.

Rusty watches Dad with undisguised curiosity. I know he wants to ask something, but he waits for Dad to finish. When Dad finishes I start, and he waits again.

"You do that every day?" he asks after I get up.

"Yup," I say with pride. "Every day. Five times."

Rusty's eyebrows shoot up. "Shit!" he says. He can't believe it. I love it when people do that. There are Muslims who don't like to show or tell people that they pray, that they fast. They are shy or embarrassed. Not me. I am proud to show people that I can pray five times a day, because I know they can't or won't do that for their God. That is, if they have one.

"What happens if you don't pray?" Rusty wants to know.

Dad looks at him with interest. "Nothing immediately," he says. "But God will find out, and you will have to pay for it one day."

Rusty's interest in prayer seems to have made Dad forget about Massoud and the meat, at least for the moment. Religion can do that to him. He will forget the meat on his own plate if he starts talking about religion.

I can see that Rusty isn't convinced. But he realizes he is getting into something that is not his cup of tea. But he is still curious.

"Are all Arabs Muslims?"

Aisha laughs so loudly that Mum has to yell from the kitchen.

"No," says Dad gravely. "Some are Shiites."

Now it's my turn to laugh. Poor Rusty is utterly confused. "We are not Arabs," I correct him. "We are Afghans."

That obviously means nothing to him. He is probably wondering in which part of Arabia Afghanistan is.

"Afghanistan is near India, north of India," Dad explains, trying to make things more specific. But it's utterly futile.

"So you're Indians?"

Now Mum has to call Aisha into the kitchen. Again. Rusty is going steadily red, not from anger but from embarrassment. He knows he has mucked up but doesn't know how or why.

"He is so cute," I hear Aisha saying in the kitchen in Dari. Mum tells her to keep her opinions to herself. I can only imagine the pout.

"My sister thinks you're cute," I tell Rusty, deciding to be cheeky. His face goes redder than the flames in the fire. Mum yells, telling me not to corrupt the boy. Corrupt Rusty?

Dad, who had been smiling at the exchange between us, now joins with some heavy stuff.

"Do you believe in God, Rusty?"

Rusty looks at Dad as if to ask whether he looks like someone who believes in God.

"Without God, your life has no meaning," Dad continues.

"Oh, Dad, leave him alone!" Aisha cries from the kitchen.

I agree with Aisha. Totally. This is not the time to convert people. The problem with Dad is that he thinks any time is God's time. I think not. There are times when you need to bring God to people, and there are times when you need to leave God and people alone. Besides, I don't know if it is a good idea to convert everybody in the world to Islam. Lots of converts to Islam I have seen are trying so hard to be even better Muslims than those who converted them that they become very boring people. Like this Aussie dude who used to come to Dad's shop to buy meat. When he was buying meat as a non-believer, he was funny, relaxed, always joking with Dad. Then he converts and, boy, all that laughter is gone, he is hardly speaking now. Only *as-salaam alaikum*, brother; thank you, brother; *inshallah*, brother. He seems to think if he laughs, God will stitch his lips together or something. But why on earth would God want a joyless disciple?

If everybody in the world becomes Muslims like that dude, we will lose a lot of fun people to God, and I can tell you there are a lot of nice people who are not Muslim. We go for these inter-faith thingies from school, and you meet loads of nice people. Christians, Hindus, Buddhists. Even Jews. Hot chicks, too. You get them all to cover up like Mum, where is the fun?

Besides, Rusty doesn't get this at all. God for him is as distant as a normal life. Dad will have to pull something special out of somewhere real quick to convince him that his life is messed up because there is no God. Dad can't. So Rusty just stares at him. Blankly, as if to ask, "So when are you gonna show me the proof?"

"Have you heard of the Koran?" Dad doesn't give up so easily. But Rusty doesn't get things that easily, either.

"What's that?"

Dad goes to the dining table and picks up the little Koran that is there. "This is our Holy Book." He gives it to Rusty. I can see Mum and Aisha standing in the kitchen, looking at him very intently. Aisha is trying hard to suppress a giggle. Mum seems amused, too, but she is concealing it better than Aisha.

Rusty looks at the book. He picks it up as if expecting it to be as heavy as a rock and seems surprised it is not. I guess he can't believe that something so little and light can be holy.

"Open it," says Dad. "And have a read. It's in English."

I just don't get this. The boy is here, holed up in our house with cops wanting his blood, and Dad wants him to read the Koran. And we don't even know if he can read that well. Little Barry's writing is not exactly Shakespearean.

And I have to say that I don't get half the stuff in it myself. Make no mistake, I am proud to be Muslim. I mean, I believe in God and have never doubted He is there somewhere watching over us, but I am a bit worried about the language in which God chose to reveal stuff to the Prophet. It's a bit like Shakespeare's English, and you really need somebody else to tell you what it means. They teach us the Koran at school, but the teacher just stands there and drones at you, making you want to do something really bad to his vocal chords. I swear, it is no wonder some Muslims become terrorists after listening to drones like that. They make God's words sound so miserable and harsh, and you listen to it enough times you will want to do something miserable to somebody. I usually ignore the drones and ask Mum and Dad to interpret the Koran. They have different styles. Dad gets all excited and starts telling us what wonderful wisdom there is in the Koran and why, therefore, we should pay very close attention to it, without really telling us what the words actually mean. I guess this is because he doesn't know half of it himself, but he believes in everything without question. Mum, on the other hand, explains things, even though she, too, can be a bit mysterious sometimes. Like when you ask her what *jihad* is all about, she says it is all about first fighting evils in your heart before going around blowing up people. When you ask her if it is okay to blow up people after declaring victory over the evils in your heart, she says by then you should know whether it is okay or not. I guess Dad and Mum are both like salesmen when it comes to interpreting the Koran, but with different styles. Dad says what a wonderful product it is, and Mum simply explains how it works. And like any good salesman who doesn't really know how it works, Dad often asks his boss: Mum.

Now Dad is offering the product to Rusty. He seems interested, but in the vague and cautious

way of kids who rarely read books. It looks interesting, but you are not sure you really want
to spend your time learning a new skill just to
read it.

"What's in it?"

"All good stuff," says Dad. "Everything you
need to live your life well."

Rusty is not convinced. He holds it up like he is
weighing it or something. "That's it?"

From the kitchen, Aisha breaks out into loud
laughter. This time Mum doesn't stop her. She
can't, because she is laughing, too.

Rusty is still confused, but he looks relaxed.
Suddenly, he starts laughing. For the first time. He
hands the Koran back to Dad.

"For a second, I thought you were serious."

Now it's my turn to laugh.

Poor Dad is left aghast. He has been trying hard
to get the boy interested in Islam, and he thinks
he is kidding!

"Philistine!" he mutters in Dari and puts the
Koran on the coffee table.

That's one great thing about Dad, though. He
is passionate about religion but in a very Aussie
way. He is passionate enough to try and convert

every non-Muslim he meets, but he is also laid back enough to leave them alone when he realizes they don't give a shit, which is very often.

"It's your fault," says Mum. "Why try to convert him now? He is trying to get away from the police. He has no time for God."

"Any time is a good time for God," says Dad, perhaps for the millionth time in his life. He reminds us that it is the duty of those who give refuge to the non-believer to enlighten him before taking him to safety. But Mum reminds him that there are non-believers and then there is Rusty.

Thus ends Dad's little effort to save Rusty's soul. Now we need to focus on the more immediate challenge: getting his body out of here before the cops get their hands on it.

8 For the next few hours, we sit and think. Around three, Mum makes some tea and brings it out with some biscuits and cake. Rusty gobbles up the food but asks for a Coke instead of tea. Mum says we have no Coke but only Pepsi. Rusty has no complaints and washes down two large pieces of cake with half a bottle of Pepsi.

Everybody knows we have to do something to get Rusty out, but nobody knows how. We are all beginning to realize that it is one thing to say it is against our religion to give up a fugitive, but it is something else to decide what to do with him. Teaching him about Islam is not going to help. We have to find way to get him to safety. But how?

Outside, the cops are quiet. Now and then we hear the chatter of a police radio. But that is all. I guess they are also thinking the same thing, how to get Rusty out. The negotiator is gone now or is at least out of sight. I guess she didn't want to hang around too much after being threatened by Rusty. Perhaps she was pretty new to the job. Maybe it was her first job or even part of her training. Who knows what cops do?

But Mustafa is still there. Hanging around, watching the house as if he were part of the police force. We can see the cops talking to him, probably finally telling him that he is not, that he is actually an irritating little prick, but I am sure Mustafa pretends he doesn't understand. He is very good at that sort of thing. He was telling Dad one day that when telemarketers call, he simply says, "No speaka tha English," and they hang up. Good tactic with telemarketers. But it may not work with cops.

We first ask Rusty if he has any ideas. He shakes his head violently. I think he just wants to get out. He doesn't want to think how. He sits there, quiet, nervous, staring at the fire. Not really sulking but moody. I guess the stress is beginning to get to him, if it hadn't got to him already.

"Do you have some place to go to?"

Rusty shakes his head. I can see it's hard for him to speak.

It would be for me, too, if I were stuck with coppers around me with nowhere to go.

Dad sighs deeply and looks at Mum again. Mum is not looking at him. She is looking at Rusty, and I can see that she has no answers, either. There is loads of compassion only a mother can give but no answers.

"Why don't you give yourself up?" Dad asks. "I am sure they will take everything into account." I think he is getting quite desperate now as he realizes how serious the whole thing is. It is one thing to stand up for your religion and culture, but getting Rusty out of the circle of cops is something else. Maybe Dad is thinking the only way out is for Rusty to go out, voluntarily. He is trying hard not to make it sound as if we were tired of him. It is lame, I know. We don't want to give him up because it is not right, but we want him to give himself up so that we get rid of him without hurting our conscience. But I, too, feel it is more honourable for all of us, considering that we can't think of anything else.

"We can give evidence in your favour," I say, trying to soften the blow. "We will."

And I mean it. We can say that he was truly distraught and hurt and that he never really meant us any harm, all of which is true.

But Rusty sees through it.

"So you want me to go out with my hands up, but you won't call the cops in?"

Dad looks at Mum as if he were a little kid caught watching an adult movie, and Mum is shaking her head. She is clearly disappointed with Dad and me.

Rusty looks worried. Mum's head-shaking reassures him but only a little. I think his confidence in us has suddenly taken a dive. He looks at Dad like he thinks Dad is about to hand him over to the coppers. Then he looks at Mum, and I can see the pleading in his eyes. The tears can't hide it. But there is also something else in those eyes. Anger. Pure and simple.

"Where the fuck is ya God now?" he asks, turning to me. "You pray to him, and when is he gonna fucking deliver?"

That stings, I can tell you. Here we are blabbering about how great God is, and He is not done anything much to help us. I am sure God is trying his best, and it is we who are failing him. I remember once this Aussie bloke at footy asked whether God sends an SMS when he wants to tell us something, and one of my Lebo mates, Bashir, said, "Yes, he does, but if your fucking phone is full of unnecessary messages, you won't get anything, and God will send the message somewhere else." I guess that is what is happening now, too. We are not thinking right for God to help us. But that sort of explanation wouldn't make any sense to Rusty right now, even though Bashir's comeback shut that bloke up real quick. No point in giving him the standard "God works in mysterious ways crap," either. Under the circumstances, God's behaviour must appear so mysterious that it probably seems like a bad joke to him.

But the response comes from Mum.

"Tell him we are not going to hand him over," she tells Dad firmly in Dari. She knows what Rusty is thinking. And her tone says that if anyone has given up on God, it's not her. Rusty can think whatever he wants of God.

Rusty looks at Mum, and even though his understanding of Dari is as bad as his understanding of God, he gets it straight away. God may not be with these jokers, but this woman is with me.

Dad reaches out and touches Rusty's arm. I think he is feeling very embarrassed about the whole thing, just like I am. "We are not going to hand you over," he translates softly. "If you don't want them to take you, we will find a way for you to slip out in the night."

That was the first indication of anything like a plan to deal with the situation. But still it's far from a real plan.

Dad looks at his watch. Five thirty. Then he looks at Mum.

"It will be dark soon," Mum tells Dad. "Then we can try."

Dad translates. That makes Rusty a bit composed. Only a bit. He wants to know how we are going to get him out.

"We will have to think of something," Dad says. But it's clear he doesn't know.

We really need to have a serious discussion. We wait for Mum to finish what she is doing in the kitchen so that we can all discuss this together. Everybody is silent. The stupid clock resumes its irritating ticking, and outside an equally annoying police radio chatters. Occasionally, Mustafa's voice is heard but not clearly enough to understand what he is saying. In the kitchen, we hear pots and pans rattling gently as Mum finishes her work.

Rusty is still staring at the fire. I hope he is not thinking of following the phones. It's not that bad.

Mum finally comes out, wiping her hands on a serviette. As Rusty has no ideas to offer, we discuss things among ourselves, in Dari because of Mum.

And as we start discussing, Rusty stands up.

"I wanna take a shit," he says, in the same tone he said he wanted to take a leak a few hours ago. We nod. We have no objections to him taking a shit. But in the toilet. It's enough he's shot the sofa.

While Rusty is in the toilet, we discuss. Gradually, we all come up with ideas. Aisha has the lamest. Get Rusty to hide somewhere in the house, she says. Tell the cops he ran away. And how are we going to convince the cops that he has run away when they are all over the place watching us? Well, she says, when they can't find him in the house, they will have to believe that he is gone. And where are we going to hide him? She doesn't know.

My idea is not brilliant, either, but I think it's better than Aisha's. At least more creative. Get Rusty to dress as a Muslim girl, wearing full *bur-ka*. There are a few in the cupboard that would fit him, from Mum's younger and slimmer days. He is tall, yes, but tall Afghan girls are not unheard of, especially when you think that Aisha isn't all that short for a girl. The cops won't get him to undress, I say confidently, but Dad and Mum shoot my idea down to Aisha's great delight. They will get a female to check, they say. And they will check thoroughly. Aisha sticks out her tongue, thrilled by my defeat.

Mum and Dad have similar ideas. Wait till it's dark and then get Rusty to slip out and hide in the hedge that runs around the house. Then he can gradually creep along the hedge towards the hedge on the side near the fence and, when he gets there, climb the fence and jump into the neighbours' garden. After that, he will have to find his way. Only Mum thinks he should move out at the back, and Dad thinks he should do it from the front. I reckon it doesn't really matter. The hedge runs all around the house, and the front- and backyards are both full of big bushes. Plenty of places to hide. We will leave only the light in the lounge so that there will be plenty of shadows in the garden.

We all reckon it's a good plan, well, at least the best we have, short of digging a tunnel. And unless, of course, there are cops creeping along the hedge. Or Mustafa for that matter. That would be a terrible experience. For both Rusty and Mustafa.

We wait for Rusty to come out so that we can discuss the plan with him. It's already dark. But Mum and Dad reckon we should wait a couple more hours until it's like eight before Rusty makes a move. And pray that the cops won't make a move before that.

We wait for Rusty. Outside the cops are waiting, too. I am sure they have begun to get uneasy, probably guessing that Rusty might pull off something in the dark.

I see some even have night vision glasses. It's not a good sight. But we have to take a chance.

"What if the bastards see him?" Dad asks, without looking at anybody in particular, but we all know it is directed at Mum. We suddenly realize that we only have Plan A. We probably need to have a Plan B and C as well.

We start thinking again, and suddenly Dad comes up with an idea. "If they see him," he says, looking at Mum, "he can creep right back in, and we will think of another plan."

That is not really a backup plan but under the circumstances better than nothing. We agree, hoping it will never happen, but knowing that if it did, we will probably take him back. Now not so much because of the Koran, but because he is Rusty.

The clock says it's six thirty. Loudly.

Rusty is still in the toilet. Almost half an hour now. Must be one big-ass dump. We can't wait for him to come out so that we can discuss the plan with him. What is the point in having a plan if he doesn't agree? But he seems more interested in cleaning his bowels.

"Go and see what he is doing," Dad says. I get up, hoping that I am not required to look inside the toilet. Aisha giggles, as if reading my mind.

I stand outside the toilet door. There is no sound. Has he gone to sleep on the toilet seat? Possible, considering how tired he was. I know sometimes Dad goes to sleep there, and one of us has to bang on the door to wake him up. So I try the same tactic. I bang on the door.

No response.

I bang again, louder this time.

"What are you doing?" Dad shouts. "Are you trying to break the door? I asked you to see what he is doing, not to break the door!"

But I can't see what he is doing, and he is not answering. Dad looks at Mum and then back at me. I bang again, still no response.

"Rusty!" I call. "Rusty! Are you there, mate?"

No response.

Suddenly, we are all worried. Has something happened to him? A heart attack maybe. I know he is too young for that kind of thing, but who knows! All that stress could have got to him. Quite possible. Maybe he was too young for all the stress. Who knows?

Or could it be that the cops did something? There is a little window in the toilet with louvers in it. Maybe a sniper shot him. Silently. Clean through the louvers. Cops can do that sort of thing. I hope it is not that bad, but it makes me bang on the door even harder.

Now Dad, too, comes and bangs on the door.

"Rusty!" he says in a loud whisper. "We have a plan to get you out. Open!"

No response.

I look at Dad. I am really worried now. Totally. Not only me, but Dad and Mum, too, and Aisha, who has now left her demarcated area to arrive at the toilet.

"Stay away," Mum growls. Must be wondering if the boy is in the toilet with his pants down. That would be *haram* beyond belief.

"Nothing else to do but break the door," I say to Dad.

He looks at Mum again as if to ask if this is really necessary. We have already lost a flat-screen TV, computer, and our phones. What is a toilet door after that? Mum shrugs her shoulders. She must be wondering if Dad has any special powers to see inside the toilet without breaking the door.

Dad and I put our shoulders to the door and push it hard. It doesn't move. A couple more pushes and it creaks. Then one more push, and the whole thing comes off with a loud noise that would have been heard by the cops outside.

We are inside the toilet, but there is no Rusty. There is a big dump in the toilet but no Rusty. Dad is staring at the dump as if that were what has become of Rusty. He keeps staring at it until Mum taps him on the shoulder and points to the window.

The window is wide open to the night. The louvers are gone. I see them in a corner of the toilet, stacked in a neat pile.

We realize what has happened. The little prick has gone through the window. Taken the louvers off and vanished. We don't know what he used for the job, but he has done it well. I am sure he had done stuff like that before. Or somebody must have taught him in prison. You learn a lot in prison.

"Bloody bastard!" gasps Dad. "He's vanished!"

I stand there imagining that long, skinny body snaking through that opening. Must have been hard, but he made it. He must have been tired of waiting and must have seen the window when he was taking the leak before. So he took the chance of wriggling out the only way he thought was safe. The SMS from God finally came! Not to us, but to Rusty. God does work in mysterious ways. If only Rusty were here for me to rub his nose in that eternal truth!

But where could he have gone after that? Was he following our plan even without knowing it? What other plans had God revealed to him? We could only guess. And we could only pray that he would not get caught.

"Bloody bastard! Bloody bastard!" That is all Dad keeps saying.

"*Hamdulillah!*" says Mum. "I hope he is all right."

Then she wrinkles her nose.

"What a horrible smell," she says, glancing at what Rusty has left behind. "Flush that thing!"

But before I can do it, there is a loud noise outside, like someone banging on the front door. Then the back door as well.

Then before we know it, they are all inside. Cops! Everywhere! Screaming for us to get down on the floor.

We are all down on the floor except Mum, who has quickly covered her face and is staring at the cops. I can't believe this. She is defying the cops now. But Mum, these are cops, not Rusty. They will shoot.

But they don't. A female cop goes up to her and shows her the sofa and asks her gently to sit down. Maybe they realize it is not good to press their luck with Mum. Those eyes look terrifying. They are pleased that at least we are on the floor, even though Dad is saying, "Bloody bastard." He probably means the cops now.

"Shut up!" one of the cops tells Dad. Dad shuts up, even though I am sure he is muttering bloody bastards under his breath. It takes a while for the bastardization to subside.

"Look in the rooms, look everywhere," a cop tells another cop. They are looking for Rusty. That is a good sign. It means they haven't got him. And they are never going to find him inside the house.

And they don't. "He is not here," one cop says to the boss cop, who is walking around like a general inside a captured enemy camp. But he looks worried. He knows he has captured an empty camp.

"Where is he?" the boss bloke asks Dad on the floor.

"Gone!" says Dad simply. "I would have told you and spared you a lot of trouble, but you asked me to shut up," he says.

"Gone?" the boss bloke echoes. "Where?"

That is what we'd like to know, too. But we don't. So we just show them the window in the bathroom.

"Through there," Dad says. He even makes a whooshing sound to show how he thinks Rusty must have gone through the window. Like a rocket.

"Gone!" Dad says again. "The bloody bastard!"

The cops are all over the toilet. I can see them from my position on the floor. They look through the window. Some go out and look in through the window like a big police peekaboo game. Some of them are staring into the pile of shit, wrinkling their noses. They are probably thinking the same thing Dad was thinking.

Above us, we can hear the stupid chopper again. Hovering around, looking for a Rusty who is not there.

And cops are not the only ones playing peekaboo. There is Mustafa, too, poking his face in through the front door. How he managed to get there I haven't got a clue, but I guess the cops lost track of him when they broke in.

We are standing now. We have been given permission. We watch as Mustafa walks around look-ing at the TV and computer, clicking his tongue.

"So this is what the bastard did, huh?" he says in Dari. "*Hamdulillah*! What a waste! What a waste!"

A cop tries to tell him that he should be outside, letting the cops do the investigation, but suddenly Mustafa is a poor, ignorant migrant. "No speaka tha English," he keeps muttering in English, the whole time telling Dad in Dari that cops are just as easy to fool as telemarketers.

WE NEVER FOUND OUT what happened to Rusty. We told the cops everything that hap-pened, except how we took the gun off him and didn't want to give Rusty up. Dad told the cops that Rusty threatened us and locked himself in the toilet, and after about half an hour we decided to break the door down because we thought there was something wrong. Why didn't you tell us that he was inside the toilet, the cops asked, and Dad said we were so terrified that he would come out and shoot us all. But you were not scared to break the door down, they asked, and Dad said, yes, because at that time we knew he was probably gone. Then why didn't you call us then, the cops asked, and Dad just looked at the man the way he looks at me when I ask too many questions.

"Who has the time to think of all that?" he asked. "We were not thinking right. We are poor immigrants, not policemen."

The cops knew there was something fishy, but I guess there was nothing they could do. What could they do? Dad's fingerprints were all over the gun, but Dad said that was because he picked it up when he found it in the toilet after the kid had sneaked out. The cops probably bought that. Probably thought the stupid Muslim had no idea what he was doing.

"Why didn't the kid take the gun with him then?" the boss guy asked Dad, and Dad snapped back. "I don't know, why don't you ask him?"

The whole thing fizzled out into nothing. I mean, nobody would have guessed what had happened, and we were not game to tell anyone, even though it was most tempting to tell the media. The newspapers were all over us. We made it to the front page of *The Age* and the *Herald Sun*, and the Internet had our story for almost a day as a breaking news item. TV people interviewed us, and *A Current Affair* spent several minutes showing the terrible damage caused to our house by the "delinquent from hell."

"Were you terrified?" the woman asked Aisha and me. We nodded like we were speechless. It was pretty good acting. Dad even called Rusty "bloody bastard" several times on camera. Only Mum was immovable, as always. She spoke only in Dari and that was to say she had nothing to say. She refused to let them take a picture of her face, too. They could take one but only with the *niqab* on, and the newspaper people took one but never published it. I guess it wouldn't have looked too good to have a fully covered Muslim woman as part of the terror-stricken family. If we were being accused of holding Rusty hostage, they would have had no hesitation in carrying it. On the front page.

Even Mustafa made an appearance on TV, with Dad's mower. "Very good family, very good family," he kept saying about us. "Always helping, always helping," he chanted, showing the mower, and Dad watched him, saying, "Bloody bastard, you never put a drop of petrol into that machine."

We never heard from Rusty. We assumed he never got caught, because we know that it was never mentioned anywhere in the media. Where he went or even how he managed to avoid so many cops, we'd never know. Maybe he was a lot smarter than we thought. And God does work in mysterious ways.

But he was something else, too. The same night we noticed that something else was missing. The little Koran! It was on the coffee table near the sofa, and now it was gone! Nobody had taken it after Rusty gave it back, and Dad had left it there. Nobody saw it after Rusty walked into the toilet. We can only guess that he took it with him, stuck in his dirty jeans pocket. If not, where else could it have gone? I don't think the cops would have taken it. Why should they? If they wanted to pick up a Koran, they could do it in so many places in Melbourne. They don't have to get it from a Muslim home they break into looking for a runaway Rusty. No, it had to be Rusty.

But why would he do that? We have many theories. Dad thinks he was, after all, persuaded by his conversion efforts, and Aisha thinks he took it as a souvenir. Mum thinks so, too, but I think he was probably wondering what sort of people we were. I walk into their home, threaten them, shoot their TV and computer, and abuse them. They beat me, feed me, and refuse to hand me over to the cops and say it's all because of this book. If I were in Rusty's shoes, I would want to know what makes people like that, I am sure.

And I hope he will find out soon. I hope he will read it, not leave it in some other toilet he is trying to escape from or something. And if he reads it, I hope that he will be interested in it enough to be a Muslim. And if he decides to convert, I hope he will become a good Muslim, like Mum and Dad, not one of those crazy bastards who call themselves Muslim and blow up people or one of them sad Muslims who have so much time and love for Allah that they have little of anything for anybody else.

And I know he will never be boring, Muslim or not. He threatened us, pointed the gun at Mum, shot our TV and computer, threw our phones in the fire, but he was never boring. In another setting with a half-decent family with or without God, he would have been the coolest dude. Why, I would have even loved to have him as the brother I always wanted. Along with Aisha, of course; she is too precious to lose, the little shit. He will certainly have to change his footy allegiance, though. Two supporters of Essendon can be too much to handle.

I hope he remembers us. For weeks, Dad kept calling him a bastard for not even telling us he was going, but I always felt he would have left something, other than the big dump in the toilet. Mum just said we did what we could, and we must not expect something in return from him. Allah will be the final judge.

But I know he was grateful. Weeks later when we were taking the busted bathroom door out for hard rubbish collectors to pick up, we came across some letters carved in the top corner of the inside of the door: "Thancs."

There is only one person who could have written that word like that. The son of Little Barry. Even in his haste to get out of the house with our Koran, he did not forget to leave one final mark. Maybe he carved it with the louver he removed, maybe with something else. But it was there, small but bold.

I hope he will survive freedom. I am sure he

will. Those freckles hide a pretty tough kid. And I hope we will meet him again, hopefully as a good Muslim, but if not, we will take him as he was any time. Without a gun, of course.

As-salaam alaikum, my brother! May Allah watch over you!